tl_ _
vowels
of the
earth

the vowels of the earth

in which our hero,
crypto-linguist Jeremiah Carp,
goes right over a glyph

matthew david brozik

First Printing: 2024
ISBN 978-1-954158-27-6

Designed by Renée Klumick/Hunt Smith Design

Humorist Books is an imprint of *Weekly Humorist* owned and operated by Humorist Media LLC.

Weekly Humorist is a weekly humor publication, subscribe online at weeklyhumorist.com

99 Wall Street New York, NY 10005

weeklyhumorist.com - humoristbooks.com - humoristmedia.com

HUMORIST
BOOKS
New York

For Dan Menaker and Joyce Clark

General, all-around, abiding gratitude
Lauren, Sydney & Lucas;
Jacob Sager Weinstein, Molly Schoemann,
Chris Jones & Phoebe Smith

Research assistance graciously provided by
Evan Damashek, Allan Krueger, Emily Rosenbaum,
Kendra Snyder & Peter Sokolowski

*Vague, mostly unhelpful, almost entirely incoherent
input provided by*
Randy Roosekrans & Aaron Vehling

Alien race naming
Jordan Gelber, Marc Krafft & Toby Wahl

First readers
Andrew Boer, Dallas Dickinson, Ronnie Raviv,
Emily Rosenbaum, Christina Schafer, Lucinda Shih,
Toby Wahl, Brad Waller & Daniel Werlin

Headline illustrations by
Anne Zimanski

Cover by
Hunt Smith Design

Reference/education
David Sacks, *Letter Perfect: The Marvelous History
of Our Alphabet From A to Z*

ACADEMIC TESTIFIES TO CONGRESS REGARDING GREAT VOWEL GRIFT; SPELLS END OF PUBLIC DECEPTION

PAY-E-I-O-U-LA!

Feds Stop Silly Syllabary

CONSPIRA-B-C!

Prof. Gets Letters of Discredit

CHRONICLER'S NOTE:

This account—of events that took place in a time very different from the present—uses modern spellings, for the obvious reason. This includes updated spellings of names of the persons involved. When brief written items from the past are reproduced herein, the original spellings have been retained for historical accuracy, but the texts of longer documents have been reformed.

NEW YORK CITY
LATE DECEMBER 1948

When I decided the moment was right, I turned off Second Avenue—onto Seventy-Eighth Street, as it happened; I had been walking with no destination, just walking and trying not to screw up anything else terrifically—then stopped short, wheeled about, and addressed the man in the jet black fedora as he came around the corner.

"You've been tailing me all morning," I hissed. I didn't actually grab the lapels of his trench coat, but I did point an accusatory finger at him. "I've seen you. Let me give you some advice: When you're stalking a man with one good eye, stay on his blind side."

"I wasn't trying to keep out of sight," he said, unintimidated. "Trust me: If I didn't want you to know I was there, you wouldn't have known."

"I don't trust you," I told him.

He didn't respond right away, but when he did, he said, "I respect that." It took the indignant wind out of my angry sails. "My name is Bradford," he went on. "I'm with the federal government. And I'd like to talk to you about something important."

"I've already given my testimony," I said. "Under oath," I added, unnecessarily. "I said everything important I have to say. And I even had some words put in my mouth."

"I know, professor," this government agent named Bradford said. "I was there. At the hearing. I heard it all. I even read the transcript afterward."

"You must be my biggest fan," I said. "What's so interesting about me? Is it how passionately I incriminated myself? How decisively I dug my own grave?"

"Professor," Bradford said, ignoring my histrionics, "I need your help. That is, I need someone's help, and I think you might be that someone. What you did... what you were involved in... the hoax, the scandal, the scapegoating... none of that disqualifies you. To the contrary, if it weren't for all of that, I might never have identified you as someone likely to have useful insight."

This brought me up short. I didn't know what to say to that.

"Can we go somewhere and talk?" Bradford asked.

"There's a greasy spoon I like near here," I said, "and I haven't eaten lunch yet."

"I know," Bradford said.

"Touché."

We stepped into a joint called Leo's. We seated ourselves at a booth toward the back. I let Bradford have the bench that faced the door, figuring a G-man would want to sit where he could see who came in and who went out. And for my part, I'd already been stabbed in the back several times that month, so I suppose I just didn't care if it happened again.

After we'd ordered food and coffee—light and sweet for me, black for him—I commented on a compact man sitting at the counter. He was wearing a long, white lab coat, and his feet were nowhere near the floor. His hair was white and not what you would call kempt.

"Mad scientist at three o'clock."

Bradford gave a slight laugh through his nose. "My father used to say it takes all kinds to make a world."

"My father used to say that it doesn't take all kinds, there just are all kinds."

"Your father was... from where?"

Pretty sneaky, Bradford, I thought. "Eastern Europe," I said.

"And he came here because..."

"Because it seemed like a smart thing to do at the time. Bradford, are you trying to get me to reveal treasonous leanings?"

"No," Bradford said. "We have no concerns on that point. But I do want to ask you just a couple more questions, if you don't mind. Besides English, do you speak any other languages as well?"

"If you mean 'in addition to' English," I answered, "then yes. If you really mean 'as well as,' then no."

"Words are a serious matter to you," Bradford commented.

"They used to be my career," I reminded him.

"What other languages are you comfortable with?" Bradford asked, returning to what he wanted to know, changing his question to accommodate my pedantry.

"I can read classical Latin and Greek, I'm proficient in the major modern Romance languages and have a functional comprehension of some of the minor ones—including Galician and Aragonese—and I've spent time with several other members of different branches of the Indo-European family. Asian languages are completely foreign to me, though."

"Do you speak Hebrew?" he asked me.

"I don't," I told him.

"But you *are* Jewish…?" It was a question… and it wasn't.

"I *am* Jewish. Most Jews born in this country don't speak Hebrew," I informed him. "A lot of them do speak Yiddish, though."

"Do you speak Yiddish?"

"Ikh kenen," I said. "But most of the time I don't. There'll be plenty of time for that."

"When?" he asked me. He seemed genuinely interested in the answer.

"When I'm an old Jew," I told him. The food arrived and I delivered a forkful of scrambled eggs into my mouth. When my head was down, I thought I noticed Bradford signal to someone, and I assumed he needed more coffee or another napkin. But it wasn't a waitress who came to the table. It was the man in the lab coat, and he didn't just come over, he took a seat on the bench next to Bradford.

"Hello," he said.

"Hello," I said, but I wasn't so sure.

"Professor Carp," Bradford said, "this is Doctor Martin Smith, a... specialist on my team."

"So it's a science project you're running?"

"After a fashion. It's what you professors call 'interdisciplinary,'" Bradford said. "And I thought you might as well meet Doctor Smith sooner rather than later. He's much nicer than I am. You could actually enjoy working with him."

"You know, you haven't yet told me anything about what you're working on."

At this, Dr. Martin Smith, specialist in something or other, stood up from our booth again and excused himself. "I should be getting back," he said. "It was a pleasure to meet you, Professor Carp."

"Likewise," I said as he left. Again, I wasn't so sure. When I was reasonably confident he was out of earshot, I questioned Bradford: "Smith? *Schmidt,* I should think."

"You've got a good ear," Bradford said. "Smith fled the Fatherland when he saw the writing on the wall. I know a man whose father did the same."

I was about to compliment Bradford again on making a good point, but something disturbing occurred to me.

"Hang on," I said instead. "Sch... mith was waiting here for us to arrive? You knew we'd be coming here? But... it was my idea. How did you know?"

"You had lunch here yesterday too."

Bradford handed me a card.

"Call me if you want to help," he said.

"Help whom?" I asked.

"Everyone," he said. "Including yourself."

When the man who called himself Bradford—just Bradford—had departed, I lingered at the restaurant. I had nowhere to be and nothing to do.

I called over the middle-aged owner when he passed by my table. Leo and I were friendly, and he didn't know or care about my recent troubles, public though they had been. "That funny little man at the counter. What did he order?"

Leo cocked his head to one side, then rattled it off: "French toast. Belgian waffles, sausages—"

"Italian or Polish?" I interrupted the restaurateur to ask.

"Both," Leo said, matter-of-factly. "And a Danish pastry," he added.

Typical German, I thought. *Trying to conquer Europe before noon.*

Then I realized that I was being indefensibly uncharitable. Hadn't Bradford told me that Smith had been an expatriate for many years? Smith and I probably had more in common than I would ever have guessed. Maybe Smith had fled Germany because he'd embarrassed himself there, gotten himself fired from his job and declared a pariah in his field, and needed a fresh start in a country where he was unknown. Or maybe he was simply wary of being coerced into contributing his scientific knowledge and faculties to a wholly inhuman and inhumane cause. Either was a good reason.

"What's new with you, Professor?" Leo was asking. I thought he had walked away while I was ruminating. Maybe he had and returned. Maybe I should have opened a small restaurant rather than doing all of the things that I had done to get me where I was just then: sitting by myself in a small restaurant, regretting several choices I'd made recently.

"Didn't see you for a couple of days," Leo mentioned.

"I was out of town," I told him. "I had business in Washington."

"Politics, Professor?"

"In a manner of speaking."

"Always knew you had a good head on your shoulders," Leo flattered me.

"Had my ass handed to me, Leo," I said.

"Yeah? Well, welcome back."

"Thanks."

I paid my tab and went home, where I wouldn't have to talk to anyone else for the rest of the day if I didn't want to. And I really didn't want to.

For six years and one day—from September 1, 1939, to September 2, 1945—a majority of the world's nations had been involved in a deadly global struggle, the most widespread conflict in human history. On December 7, 1941, Japan attacked the United States and European territories in the Pacific Ocean; the following day, the U.S. in turn declared war on Japan, although this country had already been conscripting men between 21 and 35 into military service since the previous fall.

On March 13, 1942, my turn came to appear for a medical examination antecedent to my being formally drafted. Although I had been, at 29 years old, a full-time university student about to complete my doctoral studies in crypto-linguistics and therefore eligible for an exemption, I had decided to be sporting, which is why I had previously registered with the Selective Service System when required. So I trudged out on a snowy day to visit the local conscription center when my presence was requested. I sat with other young men in the waiting room, where I got one or two strange looks from my countrymen, until I was called in to be seen by a doctor. My examination was brief; I was expeditiously declared unfit for military service on account of my moderately fallen arches—*pes planus* in medical Latin—and also because I was born without sight in my right eye. Interesting fact: In more recent years, several studies have analyzed the long-supposed correlation between so-called "flat feet" and physical injuries in soldiers, all of which have been inconclusive—the studies, not the soldiers—but none of which have suggested that the condition is a true impediment to service. Being blind in 50% of one's eyes, however, is.

The military physician thanked me for coming in, although I suspect he was being at least a little bit sarcastic, and told me I was free to go. I saluted him by briskly raising and lowering my eye patch and returned forthwith to academia, officially 4-F.

The irony, of course, is that the combination of one numeral and one consonant kept me from being sent overseas, where I could have been killed in battle, but then it was a vowel that came along and ruined the life I was thoroughly enjoying in 1948.

EARLIER DECEMBER 1948...

"Class," Mrs. Tuchinsky had announced to her tenth-grade students at William A. Wheeler High School, "we have a special guest today: Jeremiah Carp—*Doctor* Jeremiah Carp, I should say—whom I had the pleasure of teaching, once upon a time, in this very building, maybe even in this very room."

It hadn't been that room. It had been a different room in the same wing of the building. I didn't say anything, though. I had always liked Mrs. Tuchinsky and was loath to correct her in front of her current students. Kids, even at fifteen or sixteen years old, like to believe that the grownups who instruct them in matters of history, mathematics, science, literature, and physical education are infallible—and it's always better for the instructors if they do.

"Jeremiah is now an assistant professor of cryptology at Dreyfus College, and he agreed to come back to his old high school to tell you a little about what he does, in case any of you might be interested in a similar career. Professor Carp?"

"Thank you, Mrs. Tuchinsky," I said. "Just to clarify: I'm actually an *associate* professor of crypto-*linguistics*."

One of the boys in the class called out, "What's the difference?" I opened my mouth to answer, but before I could, Mrs.

Tuchinsky admonished, "If you have a question for Professor Carp, please raise your hand."

The boy raised his hand. "Yes," I acknowledged him. It seemed silly, because I already knew what he wanted to ask, but I appreciated the desire for decorum in the classroom. I was, after all, a lecturer of college students myself.

"What's the difference?" the boy asked.

"Well, *cryptology* is the study of techniques for communicating messages in secret so that a third party cannot understand them. If you wanted to tell your friend across the room that Mrs. Tuchinsky's slip was showing, for instance, you might pass him a note, but if Mrs. Tuchinsky intercepted that note, she'd be able to read it unless you wrote your message in some kind of code." (There were some titters at this scenario, which I felt was not too cheeky under the circumstances.) "But my field is more specific," I went on, "being the study of characteristics of languages that have potential applications in cryptology and cryptography... such as frequency data, letter combinations, universal patterns, and such. Does that answer your question?"

"Actually," the boy said, "I meant the difference between an assistant professor and an associate professor."

"Oh," I said. "Assistant professor is typically the entry-level tenure-track position. Associate professor is the next level. After this, I'll be a full professor, with tenure. Is anyone here considering a career in academia?" I asked.

No one raised a hand until enough time had passed that it was obvious that the question was no longer open, and then a girl raised hers.

"Cryptology was important in the war, wasn't it?"

"Cryptanalysis of enemy messages played a significant part in the Allied victory, yes," I confirmed.

"Were you involved with that?" a boy asked with some enthusiasm.

"I was not," I confessed.

"Why not?"

"Well," I said, "because while, in theory, frequency analysis relies as much on linguistic knowledge as it does on statistics, as ciphers became more complex, mathematics became more important in cryptanalysis—"

"So you didn't help at all?" someone asked, and I'm not entirely sure it wasn't Mrs. Tuchinsky.

"I like to think we all did our part to help—" I started to say, and I was very happy when someone cut me off.

"Is there an eyeball under the patch or just an empty socket?" This definitely came from a boy.

"There's an eyeball," I said. "But it doesn't work. It has never worked."

"Did you always wear an eye patch? Even as a kid?"

"Actually, no," I explained. "For a long time I didn't, but then all of a sudden I developed an extreme sensitivity to light—"

"Wait, aren't you *blind* in that eye?"

"Yes, but blindness is the absence of sight, not necessarily the absence of light."

"So it's not totally dark?"

"Correct. In fact, much of the time it's just the opposite. It's way too bright."

"Wow," I heard someone whisper, which prompted me to ask, "So, is anyone thinking about becoming blind in one eye?"

I was making a joke. Several of the students gasped.

"Well, Jeremiah," Mrs. Tuchinsky said, "thank you so much for coming to speak to us today. I'm sure you need to be getting back to your own students."

I would have told her that intersession had already begun and I didn't have another lecture or conference scheduled until the second week of 1949, but I got the hint.

"It was a pleasure," I said, to be polite. "Go Peahens!" I rooted, before remembering that the Peahens were the athletes of the college I'd attended. My old high school's athletes were Bulldogs. It goes without saying that I hadn't been one of them.

Before I exited the building, I made my way to the principal's office—not to go in, as I had no business there, but rather to stand at one of the walls just outside it, where there hung framed photographs of retired, deceased, or retired-then-deceased former faculty members. Most of them were as unknown to me as I stood there as they had been when I'd been a student, but in any event, I wanted to look upon the face of one man in particular: Charles Myers, my eleventh-grade Latin teacher. Dr. Myers had seemed to me, all those years earlier, to be the quintessential college professor—even though he'd been a high school teacher, and even though my actual college professors were not very much like him at all. Dr. Myers had been disheveled every single day. His clothing had always been stained. He'd never shaved well. And he'd always reeked of snuff, often with russet tobacco residue at the corner of one or both nostrils.

As a 35-year-old associate professor, I was very much looking forward to being just like him in forty or fifty years. In the photograph they would hang in my department building on campus after my retirement and/or death, I was going to look academically bedraggled, my curmudgeonly visage as much an inspiration to future crypto-linguists as my *curriculum vitae...*

The end-of-class bell rang, jolting me from my reverie. I managed to get out of the hallway before it filled with throngs of ungainly adolescents shuffling on to their next sessions of higher learning, but just barely.

"How'd it go?" Leah asked when I arrived at her apartment for dinner that night.

"My dissertation defense was less stressful," I answered, handing her a bouquet of flowers and a *challah*—with seeds, unsliced—and planting a kiss on her cheek. "At least the committee pretended to be interested in my area of expertise. I don't know if anyone less decorated than Audie Murphy would have been fascinating enough for those kids. If Groucho Marx had gone in to talk to them, they'd have asked him if his mustache was real."

Leah, who had turned away from me to concentrate on something on the kitchen counter, didn't respond right away, and then she didn't respond at all, so I said, "It's greasepaint."

"I know that," she said. "I was reading a recipe. You don't want a tablespoon of dill weed in a soup that calls for a teaspoon."

"No," I agreed. "I don't really like dill weed."

"I know that too, sweetheart," Leah said. "So why don't you go relax and read the paper while I finish cooking?" It seemed to be a red-letter day for giving hints to Jeremiah Carp.

On Leah's coffee table I found not one but two tabloids—the *Daily News* and the *New York Post*—neither of which I thought worthy of wrapping fish in. Not salmon anyway. If anyone asked, I'd tell them that it was because I, lacking an eye, found the papers' headline typefaces, lacking feet, difficult to read, but the truth was that I couldn't abide their casual styles. News reportage was a serious business, after all.

Also, their wordplay was typically atrocious.

"Why don't you tell me what's new, honey?" I suggested. Evidently, this was the right thing to say, because Leah was full of items to relate, though most were variations on a theme.

"Barbara is pregnant," Leah told me.

"Really?" I said. "That's wonderful."

After a pause, Leah said, "So is Sylvia. And Dorothy."

"No kidding?" I said. But Leah might not have heard me, because she wasn't finished.

"Also Marilyn."

"Anyone else?" I asked, half-sarcastically. It was a mistake. Not the half-sarcasm. The asking. And I immediately regretted it.

"No," Leah said flatly. "No one else."

And I knew just what she was saying, even though she wasn't saying it. She wasn't carrying a child. She wasn't even married yet. All of her friends were much farther along in establishing their enviable domestic lives. Leah, however, was the one they were making envious.

"Leah," I called, "do you want to get married?"

She came into the living room, wiping her hands on her apron. "Are you asking me? Is this how you're asking me?"

"I'm asking if you... want to get married. If you want us to be married. I'm not asking you, right now, to marry me, no."

"Oh," Leah said. "Of course not. I mean, of course you're not asking me right now. Not like that. But... yes, I would like to get married. I would like us to get married. Yes."

"Because we've never talked about it, you know," I said.

"I know. But we're talking about it now."

"That we are," I acknowledged. "And, just to continue the conversation," I said, following her back into her kitchen, where she resumed preparing what would be our dinner, "you would like to have children? I mean, you would like us to have children? Together?"

"I would, Jeremiah. I think it would be very nice if we had children. Together. Taste this." She put a spoon of broth up to my lips. I tasted it. It was delicious and I told her as much. "Wouldn't you like children?"

"I think I would," I said. "Sure. I just..."

"You just...?"

We had never discussed this—indeed, I'd never discussed this with anyone—so it took some effort for me to say it aloud, to the woman I was inching closer to possibly marrying and having children with.

"I would be afraid... of passing on my condition," I said, finally.

"You have a condition?" Leah asked, and I saw that she was not joking, which I was grateful for.

"My eye," I said. "I'm blind in one eye, you know."

"I know," Leah said. "I guess I just never thought of it as a condition. Is that really something you could... pass on?"

It was a genuine question, and it made me realize that I didn't know the answer. "I think it must be," I said, but I wasn't sure. "I guess we could talk to a doctor and find out. You know, before we started making babies."

"And what if we had half-blind babies?" Leah asked. "Would you love them any less?"

"What? No! Of course not," I said. "I would just..."

"Feel bad for them?" Leah guessed.

"I... I don't..."

"Did your parents feel bad for you?"

"I don't know. Maybe. A little. They never told me they did."

"Did your parents tell you that you could grow up to be whatever you wanted?"

"They did tell me that," I recalled. "As much as anyone else's parents did, probably."

"And you became..." Leah said. "A..." she added, and I realized that she was prompting me. I sighed inwardly.

"A crypto-linguist," I said.

"And is that what you wanted to be?"

"Not when I was a kid, no," I said. "But I have no regrets as an adult."

"Well," Leah said, "I would be more concerned that any child of ours would grow up to be a crypto-linguist than that he or she would be born half-blind."

"Really?" I asked.

"Really," Leah said. "Because a half-blind child can grow up to be anything. But a crypto-linguist," she remarked, "is probably going to stay a crypto-linguist."

I laughed. "While I'm a little insulted," I said, "I can't argue with your logic."

"Good. Don't," Leah said. "Go wash up instead. Dinner's just about ready."

Later that night, in my own apartment, in my own bed, in the dark—where it didn't much matter how many good eyes I had—I stared into the blackness and thought about my conversation with Leah.

Marriage. A legally or otherwise formally recognized union of two people as partners in a relationship, ideally for life. When a man leaves his mother and father and becomes one flesh with his wife, according to the Torah. Of course, my father had already left us for more heavenly pastures, in a manner of speaking, but my mother was still with me. And I knew that she, too, would have liked to see me married.

There's a word in Yiddish—*beshert*—that means "soulmate." More or less. Generally speaking, it means *meant to be. Inevitable. Preordained,* even. So some of us spend a good deal of time and energy looking for our *beshert.* Others just find a person they want to be with forever and spend time and energy *making* that person their *beshert.* Because that could work too. Preordination is a funny concept.

Of course, after getting married I wouldn't be merely a husband for very long, I knew. I'd be a father, God willing, and possibly several times over. A father. *Me.* The absent-sighted professor. Weren't parents supposed to have eyes in the backs of their heads? I didn't even have the right number in the front!

And what if, God forbid, Leah and I did have a child more like me than like her in the vision department? Would he and I ever be able to throw a ball around? Did they have father-and-daughter three-legged, two-eyed races? Would other children be cruel?

Seriously. Would other children be cruel? I'd had it not too terribly growing up, in part because I was often able to make other kids laugh, usually by making jokes about myself before they could. "My parents should have named me Sy," I'd say. "Sy Clops." But what if my child wasn't so self-deprecating? What if my child didn't have a sense of humor? That, I thought, could be even worse than being half-blind.

I realized that my heart was starting to pound in my chest, and I was sweating. If I didn't start thinking about something else, I would *never* get to sleep. But I just couldn't stop thinking about... everything. So I got out of bed and turned on a lamp and the radio. Music having charms to soothe a savage breast and all that...

Gimme Eastern trimmin' where women are women / In high silk hose and peek-a-boo clothes / And French perfume that rocks the room / And I'm all yours in buttons and bows / Buttons and bows, buttons and bows

Eventually I relaxed again, calmed indeed by the most popular song in the country at the end of 1948, even with its odd lyrics. Several versions of that number were released that year, some better, some worse, but for my money the one that topped the charts really was the best. The Betty Rhodes recording was pretty good, but even though Betty Rhodes was herself huge many years ago, she was no Dinah Shore.

(LATE DECEMBER AGAIN...)

Bradford met me in the lobby of the American Museum of Natural History, on Central Park West at 79th Street, under the cold, hollow, uncaring reconstructed skeleton of a rearing long-dead Barosaurus defending her young from an Allosaurus, according to the exhibit plaque I read more than once while waiting. I had no idea what the G-man wanted to discuss with me, but I assumed that his "interdisciplinary" project was in some way related to the museum or something in the museum's purview. That narrowed it down to birds, reptiles, amphibians, North American mammals, African mammals, Asian mammals, mammals of New York State specifically, small mammals from everywhere, primitive mammals, primates, dinosaurs, ocean life, meteorites, gems, minerals, and Theodore Roosevelt.

"I'm pleased you could make it, Professor," Bradford said.

"I'm not very busy these days," I confessed. "Which reminds me: Can I assume I'll be paid something for helping the government with its research into the merits of speaking softly and carrying a big stick or whatever it is you're up to?"

"You wouldn't work for the satisfaction that comes from aiding mankind in a time of crisis?"

"Gristedes doesn't take satisfaction as payment for groceries," I said. "I don't think so, anyway. I haven't actually inquired."

"You'll be paid," Bradford assured me. "Money. I have a budget for consultants."

"Then lead on, Bradford," I said.

Bradford led on indeed, into an elevator off the main entrance hall. He produced a small key from an inside pocket of his suit jacket, inserted it into a lock on the cab's control panel, turned it, then pushed a button unsubtly marked "X." When the doors closed and the elevator began to descend, Bradford spoke to me again.

"You've heard of Area 51?"

"I'm afraid I have not."

Bradford knitted his brow, which was no mean feat since Bradford's brow seemed to me already to be in a perpetual state of beknittedness. "In Nevada," he elaborated some but not quite enough.

"I've heard of Nevada," I told him, but that didn't appear to make him feel any better about our exchange.

"Area 51, in Nevada," he explained, "is a top secret Air Force facility, where, some people are convinced, the government of the United States is storing and examining debris from the crash of an extraterrestrial craft in the desert in Roswell, New Mexico, last year."

"And is it?" I asked. "The government, I mean. Storing and examining extraterrestrial craft debris at that top secret Air Force facility in Nevada?"

"No," Bradford said. "We're storing and examining it here."

"Oh," I remarked. "Then what's the big deal about Nevada? Why do people think there's an alien spaceship there?"

"Because that's what we want people to believe. The rumors started when Roswell Army Air Field personnel recovered a flying disc that had crashed on a nearby ranch. The flying disc was part of a high-altitude balloon equipped with microphones being used in a top secret project to detect sound waves generated by Soviet atomic tests. The 509th Operations Group whisked away the debris—to Nevada—and the public information officer issued a statement claiming that the balloon was merely of the weather-measuring variety, although he was careful not to be too convincing. All of this was orchestrated to focus attention on Area 51. To keep attention away from Area 50," Bradford mentioned.

"And where is Area 50?" I asked, although I had a feeling I already knew.

"This museum," Bradford said, his brow unknitting slightly, "is Area 50."

And just then, as if on cue, because that's how these things typically work, the elevator doors opened again. Bradford stepped out of the cab, and I followed him.

We'd only taken a couple of steps when Bradford stopped, turned to me and asked, "You really hadn't heard of Area 51 in Nevada or the crash at Roswell?" I could see that he was disappointed, and I appreciated that this was consequential to him, but I knew it wouldn't do either of us any good for me to be untruthful.

"I'm sorry, Bradford. Everything you said in there was news to me. But now I know about it," I added, thinking maybe that would offer the other man some consolation.

"Do me a favor?" he asked. "When we're done here... when you go back to your day-to-day... would you mention it to some people? Not the part about it being a diversion, of course. But the stuff about the crash and the debris and the possibility of a cover-up... could you maybe spread the word a little bit?"

"Sure, Bradford," I promised. "I'll do that for you."

"Thanks, Carp," Bradford said. "Here's Smith now. He'll take you in. I'll be in touch."

And with that, the blue-suited Bradford returned to the elevator, handing me off to the white-coated Smith, who was extending a hand for me to shake. I shook Smith's hand.

"Professor," he greeted me, smiling. "Welcome to—"

"Area 50," I put in. "Yeah, Bradford just told me. But what is Area 50, besides a basement lab in my favorite museum?"

Smith seemed taken aback by the question. "You mean...?"

"I mean," I said, "that no one has yet told me why I'm here or what I'm here to help with or how I'm supposed to be able to help, yes."

Smith laughed. "Well, I will tell you those things, in just a moment. But didn't Bradford tell you why this Area 50 is so important?"

It was my turn to laugh. "He told me some ridiculous yarn about an alien spaceship. Honestly, I hadn't thought that man possessed much in the way of a sense of humor." I smiled at Smith, expecting him to agree with me. I saw that Smith wasn't smiling or agreeing with me.

"Professor Carp," he said. "Agent Bradford was not joking."

"You're telling me that you're examining an extraterrestrial craft here?"

"That is exactly what we're doing. And that's what we need your help with."

"My help... with that?"

"Ja," Smith said, momentarily forgetting that he was no longer German. "Yes."

"What do I know about alien spacecraft? I don't even believe in aliens, much less that they travel in spacecraft, much less that they crash their spacecraft in deserts in Nevada!"

"New Mexico," Smith corrected me. "But they do, and they did."

"I'm a crypto-linguist," I reminded the other man. "A disgraced one, at that. I have no qualifications to offer any insight into anything related to space!"

I'd told this Smith character that we were in my favorite museum, and that wasn't just something I'd said to be polite, in case the walls of the American Museum of Natural History had ears and cared about the opinions of a disgraced crypto-linguist. It was a fact: I had an unreserved affection for the place. As a boy, I'd visited as often as I could, mostly to the same handful of exhibits. And not the exhibits involving stuffed rodents or plagioclase feldspar. No, I went—as most young boys did—for the two things that crowded the imaginations of young boys in my day, as they have for time immemorial and still do today: giant extinct thunder lizards, and breasts.

The permanent exhibitions of the Museum displayed in its complementary Halls of Ornithischian and Saurischian Dinosaurs are second to none among the collections of such things in the world. Ask any man who grew up in New York City and he'll tell you: He and his friends made their way to the American Museum of Natural History at least once in their youth to admire the reconstructed fossil skeletons in those halls. But likewise not to be missed was the naked primitive woman in the Human Origins exhibit. Bones and boobs.

Of course, as I got older I learned to appreciate more and more of the Museum's exhibits for more and more of the right reasons, although I never did stop being thrilled by the towering skeletons of some of the awesomely large and curious creatures whose time on the planet had come and gone long, long before human origins had even begun. And you couldn't see *those* in magazines that your friends' fathers didn't hide as well as they thought.

What I saw that day at my favorite museum, however, was extraordinary enough to displace immense reptiles as the principal stuff of both dreams and nightmares.

"I think, Professor," Smith understated, "you are going to be surprised."

And, *Gott im Himmel,* was I ever.

(BACK TO EARLY DECEMBER...)

"Ma," I'd yelled, when I'd let myself into her apartment. "Leah wants to get married." I was yelling because I didn't want to startle my mother.

"To you? Why?"

This was not a real question, and it was not my mother asking. Rather, it was my brother, Daniel, older than me by three years. He was in our mother's living room, sitting on her couch. Reading the *Post*.

"What are *you* doing with a newspaper?" I asked. "Baseball doesn't start again until April."

"Oh," Danny said, "look who knows all about sports now!" In fact, I wasn't even sure that I'd gotten the month right, but I must have, because Danny didn't make fun of me for that. Instead, he asked, "So who's gonna win it all next year?"

I pretended to be giving the matter serious consideration for a minute or so—but I was really just trying to remember the name of any team that wasn't from New York. When I couldn't, I said: "The Yankees."

"Over who?"

"Brooklyn."

"All right, Germy," Danny said, "we'll see." Of course my older brother called me Germy.

"Dunny, who are you talking to?" *This* was our mother, calling from another room of the apartment, almost certainly the kitchen. Jewish women, young and old, were usually to be found in the kitchen, by choice.

"Germy's here, Ma," Danny called back.

"Jeremiah!" my mother cried, bounding in and receiving me in her ample, maternal bosom. "What can I get you to eat?"

"What do you have?" I asked.

"What do I have, he asks!" she said. "What do I have!"

"Well?" I asked.

"Well, go see for yourself. You're not a cripple!" *Just as I'd told Leah.*

"Okay, Ma," I said. "I'll look in a minute. But first I want to talk to you about something."

"You want to talk?" she asked rhetorically. "Then sit, sit! Sit next to your brother. Dunny, make room for Jeremiah."

"Yeah, Dummy, move over." Of course I called my older brother Dummy.

Danny moved over on the couch, causing the plastic covering to make the noise that a plastic couch cushion makes when someone moves on it. I sat, and I tried to sit still, because that noise is not a pleasant one.

"Leah wants to get married," Danny said, just as I'd opened my mouth.

"To you, Jeremiah?" my mother asked. "Why?"

Danny snickered behind the paper, which he'd resumed reading, or was simply snickering behind.

"Very funny, the both of you."

"Of course she wants to marry you, Jeremiah. Do you want to marry her?"

"I think so," I said.

Danny made a humming sound.

"What?" I asked.

Danny put down the paper. "Jeremiah," he said, "when I asked Sharon to be my wife it was because I knew that I wanted to spend the rest of my life with her, that I wanted to make a home with her, start a family with her. There was no doubt in my mind or my heart about it. If you'd asked me if I loved her, I'd have said yes three times before you'd even finished the question."

I looked at my older brother as if seeing him for the first time. "Answer this question: Are you an alien?"

"Listen to Dunny," my mother said. "If you don't love Leah, don't marry her. But if you do love her, then don't make her wait for you much longer. She won't wait," my mother said.

I thought about this, then sighed.

"Okay," I said. "I'll ask her to marry me."

"Good luck," my brother said, picking up the paper again. "She might have come to her senses by now."

"And where *is* your wife?" I asked him. "The one you can't live without. The air that you breathe, the reason you wake up every morning?"

"I didn't say any of that," Danny pointed out. "She took the twins for a walk. They'll be back soon." The twins were my nephew and niece, Abraham and Beatrice—Abe and Bea— both 6 years old, and both adorable and precocious, clearly taking after my sister-in-law.

My mother returned to the room, prompting me to realize that she had stepped out.

"Jeremiah," she said to me, with what seemed to be solemnity of a sort, "if you are going to propose marriage to Leah, then I want you to take this." My mother was holding a small, black, felt jewelry box.

"Ma."

"Take it."

I took the box from my mother. After a moment, I opened it. There was a diamond ring inside.

"Ma," I said, "this... this ring is hideous! This isn't your engagement ring..."

"Of course it's not," my mother said. "Why would I give you my engagement ring? My engagement ring is beautiful. And it's mine! Your father gave it to me."

"Yes, Ma, I know who you were married to." I looked at her hand. "But where *is* your ring?"

"It's on my dresser. It gets loose in the wintertime. I take it off so I won't lose it."

"Okay, so whose ring is *this,* then?"

"This was my aunt Pearl's ring. I got it when she finally died."

"I can't give this to Leah," I said. "She'd think I went *completely* blind."

"You're *not* going to give that ring to Leah," my mother agreed. "You're going to give her a brand new ring. But with that diamond. The ring is strictly from hunger," my mother said, "but the diamond is nice."

I laughed. "Thank you, Ma." I kissed my mother on the cheek.

"Hey, how come you didn't give me Aunt Pearl's ugly ring?" Danny asked. "She was already dead when I needed a diamond."

"You were making a nice living, Dunny." My brother was a furrier, and he did indeed make a nice living. "Jeremiah could use it more than you."

"I'm doing just fine," I told them. "And soon I'll be doing even better."

"How *is* the cryptonomy business?" Danny asked. "Cryptoscopy?"

"Crypto-linguistics," I reminded him, not for the first time. "You know what I do!"

"Jeremiah," my mother said, pinching my cheek, "you're a good son and a good brother, and you'll make a good husband and a good father. But nobody knows what it is that you do. Now let's all go to the kitchen and get something to eat."

Of course I knew that I wanted to spend the rest of my life with Leah. At least, I thought I knew I did. But how would I *know* that I knew? I supposed I'd... just know. And as soon as I knew that I knew, I'd ask her to marry me, I promised myself.

And as soon as I could make my brother look like an idiot again, I would do that too, I promised the Universe.

Sure enough—and soon enough—that night, once again in bed and staring into the dark, I had an appropriately mischievous idea.

(BACK TO LATE DECEMBER AGAIN...)

Smith had brought me into a... well, a subterranean science room is the best way I can characterize it. It was too-brightly lit by overhead fluorescent lamps; there was a large, flat, empty, stainless steel table in the middle of it; and on workbenches and shelves arranged against its walls were every manner of... these and those, which I imagined did this and that, all in the name of the intellectual and practical activity encompassing the systematic study of the structure and behavior of the physical and natural world through observation and experiment. That is to say: science.

On a side bench was one of the few devices I recognized. Smith went over to and then employed it, lifting and then speaking softly into its handset. A moment later, a young woman entered the room with a black case, which she placed on the large central table. Smith thanked her, and she departed again. Although my eye was on the case, she hadn't failed to catch it. My eye, I mean. Figuratively. Her figure, I mean. I might have begun to be actually distracted by her more than just in passing, but then Smith opened the case, which had his full attention and soon claimed mine as well.

"Have you seen the dinosaur exhibit upstairs, Professor?" Smith asked me.

Had I seen the dinosaur exhibit? Really?

"Best part of the whole museum," I remarked.

"What do you find most... impressive about the exhibit?"

I knew the answer. That is, I knew what Smith wanted me to say, which is not that giant reptiles are simply unbelievably awesome. So I answered: "That we've been able to extrapolate what some prehistoric creatures looked like by examining only a single fossilized toenail, or tooth, or tail spike." By *we* of course I meant humans generally, not any set of them that included me specifically.

"Yes! Exactly right!" Smith agreed. "Well, we are doing the same thing here, only for a machine instead of an organism." (By *we,* I understood, Smith did mean himself and others, specifically.) "What was salvaged from the crash in the desert is not much, but we are making progress. It is just very slow going, because it is like trying to reconstruct a thousand-piece... how do you say, *Zusammensetzspiel?*

"Jigsaw puzzle," I offered after a moment's worth of consideration and recollection.

"Yes, like trying to reconstruct a jigsaw puzzle from only one piece. Also, we are only guessing that it is a thousand-piece puzzle. It could have two thousand pieces. Or ten thousand! And yet, by analyzing what we have—the shape, the size, the markings—we might get some sense of the overall design."

"One piece?" That was far fewer than I'd assumed had been recovered.

"One piece," Smith confirmed. "And small," he added, inclining his head toward the case on the table.

"I take it there was no... one in the craft who could tell you what it looked like and how it worked?"

"It was a craft unmanned, if you will pardon the expression. As far as we can tell."

I was trying to imagine how difficult the task of reconstructing an alien spaceship would be, having no idea what it looked like intact, in possession of only a presumably scorched and likely mangled piece of debris to work with: trying to put that piece into place in an indeterminate arrangement, and with no picture on a box to look at for reference. Indeed, not even a recommended age range.

"You said 'markings.' Internal markings?" I asked. "Like control panel labels? Or external markings, like... racing stripes?"

"External, we think." Smith said. "Not racing stripes, though."

"But decorative?" I asked. "Or functional?"

Smith began to smile. "Possibly both," he said, adding, "we think."

I was beginning to understand how I might be able to help. At least, how Bradford and Smith and maybe others thought I might be able to help.

"Language?" I asked. For all I knew, alien spaceships could display alien brand names or alien pinups.

Now Smith was smiling, undeniably. He seemed almost giddy, as if he—or I—were on the verge of a truly momentous discovery, or realization. "We think so," he confirmed. So that was it. They wanted my help making sense of what they thought were alien words.

"I'm not fluent in extraterrestrial, though," I said.

"You might not need to be," Smith said—rather cryptically, it seemed to me, and I had a keen eye for cryptic.

"Why not?" I asked, suddenly uncomfortably aware of what the hairs on the back of my neck were doing.

"Now is as good a time as any for you to see for yourself, Professor." Smith beckoned me over to the examination table, to the open black case, to look at what was inside. I went, but not without hesitation. Was I really going to see something from outer space? Something built by intelligent creatures from somewhere other than Earth? Something that told us for certain that we, humans, were not alone in the Universe? Something that only a select handful of others on this planet had seen?

What I saw when I finally did look into the case on the table made not much of an impression on me at all, initially. In a bed of dark felt was a tarnished scrap of a bluish gunmetal, twisted and charred on two edges. It could have come from something manufactured in Detroit, or the Brooklyn Navy Yard. But then I saw the markings Smith had spoken of. I realized that I was making out individual characters... letters. I realized that I *recognized* the letters, moreover. I was familiar with those letters. All of them. I *shouldn't* have been able to recognize all of them, though.

But...

Oh.

Of course.

I considered not reacting—not outwardly, that is; not giving this strange little foreign man I'd never seen before that week the satisfaction, but the best I could do was to contain my outward reaction for what I suppose was maybe half a minute but was probably much less.

"Go to hell, Schmidt," I spat out, finally. The uneasy sensation on my nape was replaced by a hot one in my face. "You and Bradford both." If the small man was laughing, I didn't hear it.

I walked—mostly calmly, to my credit—away from the table and out the door of the examination room. Not so much to my credit, once outside the exam room I nearly knocked over the young woman who had brought in the case, but I was too ticked off to apologize. On the other hand, maybe she had been in on the joke, in which case she could join the party going to hell.

I almost—*almost*—didn't notice how good she smelled. I was that angry.

I'm no stranger to playground cruelty. I've been blind in one eye since birth, and anything that makes a child different makes him a potential target for the taunts and insults of his playmates. Because little kids are schmucks, for the most part. One tends to expect more, though—that is to say better treatment—as an adult from other adults, and certainly from other serious professionals, even professionals in disciplines different from one's own.

Maybe, not unlike my bad eye, I was being overly sensitive to light—in this case light being made of my recent disgrace. But by strangers. If my family had wanted to tease me, I'd have reacted differently, probably—but none of them had, as it happened. Either they were too polite or, more likely, too ashamed, but in any event no relative seemed interested in talking—to me— about what I'd done and what had done me in. Yet here were a purported government agent and wise old German scientist— both seemingly straight out of central casting—who had evidently gone to great lengths to mock me. Come to think of it, though, *were* they actors? Had someone hired them? Was I wrong about my family? Was this their payback for the football score trick?

Was Leah involved?

I found myself hoping so, if only so I could speak to her again. And tell her that I wasn't laughing. It was just too soon. Or was I fooling myself thinking that I'd ever be able to see the humor in it? On the other hand, I'd probably found amusement in greater tragedies. Just not any of my own, of my own doing, more or less. At the same time, as much as I wanted to believe that Leah would have been willing to joke about recent events, I knew that she wouldn't be. And that only compounded the tragedy. When it came down to it, I didn't have a true friend in the world any longer. I'd let myself be fooled into thinking that maybe I was making some new ones, or at least some new colleagues, but I'd been wrong about that too.

(EARLY DECEMBER ONCE MORE...)

Even though it was between semesters, I'd popped uptown—way uptown—to my office at the college, for a change of scenery. Really I was just going to read the newspaper there, rather than in my apartment. I didn't expect to see anyone else on campus. In any event, I wasn't counting on running into anyone I knew. But I suppose I'd hoped that I would; I enjoyed the company and camaraderie of my collegiate colleagues.

So I was leaning back in my wooden chair on wheels, feet up on my desk like a dime-novel private eye, reading the *Times*. I'd made it all the way to page seven before an article made me angry.

SENATE UNIT NAMES SONNETISTS AS PURPLES, ran the headline, with the subhead **Pair Accused of Membership in an Atonic Repetition 'Cell' During Wartime Work.**

WASHINGTON, December 6 — The Senate Committee for Unimaginative Activities said today that Dr. Geoffrey Royce Lanham and Dr. Theodore Wain, both atonic syllabists, had belonged to a wartime Sonnetist cell at the repetition laboratory at the University of California at Quirkeley in the early part of the decade.

Dr. Wain is now a phonetics professor at Vandeventer University. Dr. Lanham until recently was on the faculty at Dreyfus College in New York City. Each appeared before the committee, and each refused to answer questions about Sonnetist connections on grounds that he might incriminate himself.

I knew Geoff Lanham. At least, I'd met him before he'd retired from Dreyfus, where he was still professor *emeritus,* and I was familiar with his work on unaccented syllables. I'd heard him speak more than once on his quest to discover an alternate verse without any stress. Reading that Lanham was being accused of being a "Purple"—one whose otherwise serious professional work was infused with just too much elaboration or ornamentation for the liking of some of the more staid and suspicious Powers That Were—disturbed me to no end.

Not, of course, because I didn't want to believe that he was a Purple, but because it meant that the Purple Scare was not just continuing but deepening, with suspicious eyes peering into more industries and disciplines. This accusation hit entirely too close to home, literally. Dreyfus College was my second home— heck, I was there even when I had nothing to do there, when I could have been at my first home, in my pajamas—and if Senator McBeth's cynical cronies were questioning—attempting to question, anyway—former professors from my institution, then who knew just how circumspect those of us still teaching there would need to be. Though disgusted, I read on.

Today's report said that the alleged Quirkeley cell had been organized by one Stephen Field, whom it described as a Sonnetist Party worker in western Pennsylvania. Mr. Field was also a witness and refused to answer questions.

The committee named the men in a foreword to an official document in which it published its hearings on

Mr. Field. It said it was still checking on other alleged cell members.

Dr. Wain said today at Vandeventer that he had no comment on the committee's announcement. Vandeventer issued a statement last May in which it said that Dr. Wain was not engaged in secret work there, stating further that he had been regarded by his colleagues as a "thoroughly serious man and at no time has there been any reason for questioning his dedication to the conventional."

Dr. Lanham was not available for comment today.

Shame on you, Vandeventer, I thought, putting the paper, my feet, and that other school down. *Good for you, though, Geoff. I hope you're... wherever you want to be, doing whatever you want to be doing. You earned a peaceful retirement. You don't deserve to be persecuted. None of us does, really. Probably.*

I was now too wound up to even remain seated, so I got out of my chair and left my office, headed nowhere in particular. I thought a stroll through the empty building that housed the Linguistics and Domestic Languages departments would help clear my head of the unkind thoughts I was having.

"Carp!"

Someone was calling my name. I looked around and spied Gil Silver—originally Silverrod—a literature professor about my age. He was also walking the halls, and he seemed perturbed as well.

"Gil," I said. "Nice to see you." It really was. "Wife kick you out of the house?"

"She didn't have to," Gil said.

"I understand completely," I said.

"Do you? Did you get married since last week," Gil asked, "or are you still happy?"

I chuckled. Then I said, "You heard about Lanham? I was just reading the *Times* article."

"I heard," Gil said, "and I've even tried calling him. No luck. He must be lying low. I just hope he's got enough good Scotch wherever he's hunkered down."

"You've dabbled in the arts. Are you at all afraid that you might one day show up on the wrong committee's radar?"

"I wasn't until you suggested it," he joked. At least, I thought he was joking.

"Well, if I'm ever asked to name names," I assured him, "I'll make sure to have trouble remembering yours... Bill."

Gil laughed. "You're a good man, Jeremiah Carp. A good man and an even better American. I'm going to head out. You enjoy the rest of the break, and I'll see you next year."

"Be well, Gil," I said.

I returned to my office in a much better mood than I'd been when I'd left it just twenty minutes earlier. I pushed the *Times* from my desk into my wastebasket. I wasn't going to risk getting unsettled anew by something in the paper. In fact, I wasn't going to read anything else, I decided. And since my office was filled from top to bottom with nothing but printed matter, I decided it was time for me to head out again myself.

I didn't go directly home, though. I first had to stop into a post office and mail a whole bunch of envelopes.

"Christmas cards?" the clerk asked me as I piled up my stacks on the counter at his window.

"Cards," I said, but I didn't elaborate.

"Hang on," he said. "These are all addressed to the same person."

"They're all addressed to me, actually," I told the clerk. Then it occurred to me that if I left it at that, he'd only ask me more questions, so I added, "It's for an experiment I'm doing."

"You're some kind of scientist?" he asked me. At least he was stamping my mail and hand-cancelling the stamps as we were conversing.

"It's more of a... psychology experiment," I said.

"You're a psychologist?" he asked me.

"I'm a crypto-linguist," I informed the other man.

That brought him up short. Or, I thought it had.

"Ah," the clerk said. "Frequency data, letter combinations, universal patterns, and those sorts of things?"

"What?" I asked. "I mean... yes. Yes, *exactly* those sorts of things!"

"There good money in that?"

"Not as good as I'd like," I confessed.

"Maybe you shouldn't send yourself so much mail then," the clerk suggested. Before I could craft a witty comeback, he said, "Would you mind if I asked you a question about your chosen field, Doctor Carp?"

"How do you know my name?" In response, the clerk merely shifted his gaze down to the envelopes he was processing. The ones with my name on them. The ones I had just told him I was mailing to myself. "Right," I said. "Sure, ask me anything you like."

"Well, a friend of mine believes that even a small amount of gibberish, irreconcilable with the pattern of a certain language, proves that the decipherment of a block of text cannot be right for that language. I don't agree. I'm of the mind that a decipherment, being a professed solution to a particular kind of linguistic problem, cannot afford to ignore any part of any text as semantically obscure or uncertain, unless it's physically damaged and therefore phonetically doubtful.

"Which one of us is right?"

I stared at the postal clerk for what felt like a long time before I answered him. I'd meant to be marshaling my thoughts, but it was all I could do not to wonder how, and why, this young man—and his friend!—knew as much about my chosen field as they did.

"I'd love to be able to tell you that one of you is correct and the other isn't," I said finally, "but the truth is: You're both right."

"Really?" the clerk asked. "But—"

"Trust me," I told him, and when I saw that he'd finished with my mail, I said, "Happy holidays" and took my leave.

I've got no qualms about admitting that my exchange with that postal clerk improved my mood considerably. Most of the time, crypto-linguistics was a solitary specialty, so meeting someone else genuinely interested in the field—even an amateur—was a pleasant experience. I'd be lying if I said it hadn't made me feel like something of a hero, even. Someone the youth of America might look up to. Someone to give them hope in those uncertain, unstable times.

(AND NOW LATE DECEMBER YET AGAIN...)

When the elevator finally arrived in response to my repeated angry stabbing of the call button, the doors opened to reveal Bradford. To my chagrin. To put it mildly.

"Very funny," I snarled at him. "Hilarious."

"What is, Carp?"

I didn't deign to respond. All I wanted to do just then was trade places with him, to be in that elevator, with him out of it. I'd have physically thrown him out if I hadn't suspected that he could break me in half.

"Professor! Professor Carp!"

Smith had come running out of the examination room and was calling after me. He was not laughing. I waited until he had reached us at the elevator—which Bradford was now outside but still blocking—to ask them both at once, "So who are you guys really, and why would you go to this much effort just to make fun of me?"

"We're exactly who I've said we are," Bradford said. "Making fun of you isn't part of our mission."

"What you just saw is genuine, Professor Carp," Smith put in. *Genuine.* The word felt like a punch in the gut.

A long moment passed before I said anything more. I took some time to collect my thoughts before speaking.

"You're telling me that... an alien spacecraft... that crashed in the desert in New—in Nevada," I corrected myself before either other man could, "was found marked with all or part of the Modern Roman alphabet..."

"New Mexico," Smith corrected me.

"Damn it."

"And?" Bradford asked.

"...and," I said, though I didn't want to continue, "among those letters, there is one letter that doesn't belong."

"But with which *you* are familiar," Smith put in.

"Unfortunately," I said.

"It is *not* unfortunate!" Smith asserted. "It is very fortunate indeed!"

"How do you figure? And how are you still pretending that this is... real? If this isn't *your* joke on *me,* doesn't everything about this—in light of recent events—suggest that someone is playing a joke on *you?"*

"To the contrary," Smith enthused. "Everything about it tells us that it is real. It is old, and it has been in space, beyond the boundaries of our solar system. Of this we are certain!"

"What we believe," Bradford stated, "is that the obvious presence, on the hull of the ship, of an alphabet of a centuries-old language of Earth was meant to be a message to humans that whoever built and sent the craft had been here before."

"But... but the aitch," I whispered—for among the Modern Roman letters on the piece of the ship was, unmistakably, the character at the center of my one-week-old decisive downfall.

"Yes!" Smith said. "The aitch!"

"Officially, it's called 'Glyph Two-Six,'" Bradford put in.

"There shouldn't *be* an aitch," I said, ignoring Bradford for the time being. *"There is no aitch.* We... we made it up. We invented it. Recently."

After a moment, Smith asked, "Are you certain?"

"Of course I'm certain," I said. "Look, a month ago I might have insisted the opposite—disingenuously, of course—but now that the hoax is over and done with, and my career with it, there's no reason for me to keep pretending that I did anything other than fabricate a pedigree for a made-up, new, purportedly old, letter of the alphabet. Just what I admitted to a Congressional committee only days ago. Remember, Bradford? You have the transcript," I reminded him.

"Professor," Bradford replied, with admirable equanimity, "I believe you."

"You do?" I asked.

"Yes," he said. "I do. I believe that you fabricated a history of the letter at the center of the hoax for which you were made to take the blame."

The man must keep those transcripts on his bedside table, I thought. He continued:

"I do not suspect that you had any knowledge of the actual existence of Glyph Two-Six. I have no illusions that you were aware of its presence on the wreckage of an extraterrestrial craft that crashed in a desert in New Mexico, moreover. In short," Bradford cut to the chase, "I am completely convinced that the synchrony of the mostly harmless invention of the aitch in which you played a part and the discovery of the same item on an alien spaceship in the company of the rest of our alphabet, or part of it, is simply coincidence and nothing more."

"Then why—" I began to ask, before interrupting myself: "Wait. You said you don't believe I knew about the actual existence of the aitch. Why? Wouldn't you assume that if I'd gone to great lengths to make up a pedigree for an invented letter that I was claiming had disappeared centuries ago... I'd have done my research? In the course of which, I'd have turned up anything that revealed the actual existence of the letter I was helping to invent... albeit perhaps unnecessarily, it would seem?"

"We try not to assume anything, Professor," Bradford said. "But, yes, we presumed that you had done extensive research. Exhaustive, even. And we are confident that you found no trace of the aitch."

"Because...?" My ego was trying to decide whether or not to be bruised.

"Because we've found no trace of it," Bradford explained. "The government has researchers too, you know. Very good ones."

That made sense, of course. And then I saw what Bradford's angle was, finally.

"You're baiting me," I said. "You're telling me that the government's experts have scrutinized every ancient manuscript and literally turned over every rock they've been able to get their hands on, but they've found nothing to confirm that the aitch ever existed. And yet an alien spaceship is telling you that it did, that once upon a time there was another letter. And, notwithstanding what you'd prefer, you have every reason to believe what's on that spaceship hull. So why is there no trace of the letter on Earth, you're left to wonder. Why can't your best men find it anywhere?"

Bradford kept a straight face, but I could see Smith, behind him, smiling.

"You think I'm better than the government's best men," I declared. "You think I'm the man to solve this mystery. You think I can do what everyone else has utterly, totally, and fully failed to do." In the end, my ego had decided to stroke itself.

I give Bradford a lot of credit. I probably would have socked me. But he didn't even say anything in reply. Instead, he wordlessly handed me a small black wallet. In it were an ID card granting me all-hours access to the Museum building and a key to the elevator that would get me down to Area 50.

"Smith," he said to Smith, "finish Carp's tour. And make sure he knows where the fire extinguishers are."

"You have a problem with authority, I think," Smith observed when Bradford had gone.

"It's mutual," I said.

"It is a good thing then that Bradford likes you."

"You think he likes me?"

"I might have chosen the wrong verb," Smith said. "He needs you, however. We need you. But Bradford does want to help you."

"Bradford wants me to help him. To help you. Plural," I said.

"It can be both, no?"

"Smith," I asked, "where did Bradford find *you?*"

"I'm afraid that is classified information, Professor Carp."

I laughed aloud. The scientist I was supposed to work with to analyze extraterrestrial spaceship debris was playing the Top Secret card. "Fair enough," I said. "But I'm not going to tell you my favorite color, in that case."

"It is blue," Smith stated.

"My lucky number then."

"Twelve."

"My dog's name?"

"Rascal."

"All wrong, Smith. I hope you're better at science than you are at reading minds."

"Was I supposed to be reading your mind?" Smith asked. "I was just making guesses. Let me try again."

"Maybe another time," I said. "For now I think I'll go home and..." I trailed off.

"And, Professor Carp?"

"Nope," I said. "That's as far as I can plan under the circumstances."

"I understand. The world just got much bigger for you. It is a difficult thing to take in," Smith said, sagely. "A nap might help."

"You think I'm ever going to be able to sleep again, Smith? That's optimistic."

You have a problem with authority, Smith had speculated. That stung too. Because, after years and years of dedication, hard work, and sacrifice, I'd *become* an authority in my area of study. And then, in short order, I'd managed to go from outstanding in my field to standing out in the cold.

In the comfort, quiet, solitude, and privacy of my apartment, I poured myself a drink. Back then, my cocktail of choice was gin and tonic. I dropped two ice cubes from my freezer into a heavy glass tumbler, then added gin from a bottle I took out of a cabinet. Upon discovering that I had no tonic water in the refrigerator or elsewhere, I added more gin to my glass. I also had no lime or even lime juice, so I topped off my drink with a splash of gin. Then I took it to my armchair to try to forget everything I'd seen and heard earlier that day.

It was all, in a word, unbelievable. In two words: utterly incredible. What I'd seen was absurd enough. But almost more absurd was what I'd heard: Two otherwise intelligent men— one a man of science, the other a man of... secret government activities, but for sure the kind of secret government activities that no one would put a gullible man in charge of, both convinced that what they'd been so keen to show me was the real McCoy—if McCoy was a being from another world. McCoy's remote-controlled spaceship, anyway.

I suddenly felt a need to be grounded, if you will, in reality, so I did the most foolish thing I could have done just then: I called my mother.

"Ma," I said when she'd answered the phone, "it's Jeremiah."

"I know, pussycat. Is everything okay?"

"Actually, Ma," I said, "no. Everything's not okay. I met a man this morning—"

"*Gevalt!*" I heard her whisper, except my mother was not very good at whispering.

"No, Ma, not like that. Just listen: I met a man from the government. He'd been following me."

"Again with the government, Jeremiah? Why won't they leave you alone?"

"Well, they have, Ma. This man wasn't with the others. He... he's working on a special project. He asked me to help."

"A job? That's terrific, no?"

"It's not quite a job. It's more like... like a project."

"Are they paying you to work on this project?"

"I think so."

"You think so? You don't know? You're going to work on a project for people and you don't know if they're going to pay you? You're so rich, you can afford to work for free?"

"Ma, they're going to pay me. That's not the point."

"Then what's the problem? You don't like the work?"

"It's not..." I started, then for the first time wondered how I was going to explain any of it to my mother, and why I'd thought I would be able to. "It's not that I don't like the work. It's that I don't really understand it."

"So you'll learn. In my eyes, you can do anything."

"That's nice, Ma. That's nice. But... well, what I mean is that I don't..." I tried again. "I can't..."

"Jeremiah, what is it? Tell your mother what's upsetting you."

"Ma," I said, deciding at last just to forge ahead, blurt it all out: "This afternoon I saw part of a crashed flying saucer—an honest-to-God alien spaceship—and on it, along with other letters from the Modern Roman alphabet, was the aitch. The aitch is real, and it's been real for a long time. Aliens even know about it! I was right, Ma. I was wrong, but at the same time I was right."

My mother didn't respond right away. I was afraid I was going to have to repeat myself. But then she said, quietly, "It's enough already, Jeremiah," and I could hear the grave disappointment in her voice. Literally. I could hear disappointment that was not just hers but also a generous portion that she was conveying on behalf of my late father. "I have to move the laundry," she said before I could say anything further and make things worse. "But I'll see you for dinner Friday night?"

"Sure, Ma. Sure. Dinner Friday night."

"Maybe you'll bring a friend?" she asked. She meant Leah, of course. But that didn't seem at all likely.

"We'll see, Ma. Maybe," I said. "But don't cook any extra. I love you."

"I love you too, pussycat."

So that, I thought when I'd hung up my phone, *was a mistake.* I didn't call anyone else. I just sat in silence and drank my gin and gin and gin. And I talked to my dad. Who had been dead some ten years already at that point.

"Pop, I'm in a pickle," I said aloud. "And I know how you love pickles. You probably heard my conversation with Ma. What do you think about all this?"

He didn't answer me at first or at all, but I imagined that if he had been inclined to respond, he'd have asked me if I remembered what the Talmud says about the blind men and the elephant.

"I don't think that's the Talmud, Pop... but I know the story you mean, and although I'm only half-blind, I think I see your point just the same. Okay. Thanks. Say hello to your folks for me, please. I love you, and I miss you."

I really did. My father had been fun in a way that my mother just wasn't. Some people just aren't, which is probably for the best. Otherwise, we'd all be competing to make each other laugh. Maybe. "We can't all be heroes," as the man said, "because somebody has to sit on the curb and applaud when they go by." My father had been fond of that quip—and Will Rogers generally—and I'd become fond of it, and him, in turn. My father had never been a hero, other than to his family, but he had understood the importance of recognizing the achievements of others, heroic or just human. He'd always been the first to congratulate Danny or me on anything we'd accomplished that we'd set out to do, and then to encourage us to go further, to take the next step, to try something more difficult. That's probably why I'd proceeded higher and deeper in academia and why Danny had fallen out of so many trees.

Be nice to your brother, I heard my mother say.

Listen to your mother, I heard my father say.

I sighed and sat quietly again.

Six men, all without sight, went to see—but not really—an elephant. Each touched a different part of the animal and came to a hasty conclusion about its nature from his limited perception. The first felt the animal's broad side and declared it to be a wall; the second felt the tusk and thought it a spear; the third took hold of the trunk and mistook it for a snake; the fourth thought the animal's leg was a tree trunk; the fifth grabbed an ear of the beast and called it a fan; the sixth clutched the tail and reckoned it was a rope. Then the six men argued, each one slightly right, yet all of them wrong.

Flying saucer, I'd told my mother. *Alien spaceship. Honest to God.*

I wondered if she had even for the briefest of moments considered that what I'd said might be true. My mother, I knew, would not have been keen on the idea of aliens visiting Earth, recently or in the past. The possibility of beings from another world on the planet at the same time as her would have disturbed her to no end, I was sure. But if she did find a way to believe it, I knew she would then be convinced that anyone who disagreed with her, about anything—how many eggs to put into a matzo ball mixture, the rules of canasta, which one was Laurel and which was Hardy—was from Pluto.

My father, on the other hand, would have been excited to meet an alien, to ask him, her, or it dozens of questions—hundreds, even—about anything and everything. My father had been a people person, as we say. He probably would have been an alien person as well. He would have encouraged them in their plans to conquer and enslave humanity, if they had seemed enthusiastic enough about it. "You came all this way," he'd have told the invaders, "don't rest on your laurels. Take the next step. Dream bigger. Your slimy, reptilian reach should exceed your scaly, webbed grasp..."

My brother would have called up eight friends and challenged the visitors to a full game of baseball. If his team had won, Danny would have insisted that it proved that Earth was the best planet in the entire Universe. If his team had lost, Danny would have insisted that they make it a doubleheader.

Aliens.

On Earth.

A wall.

A spear.

A snake.

A tree.

A fan.

A rope.

All right, all wrong.

Damn it.

I swallowed the last of my drink and put on my coat again. I had to go back to Area 50. I had to gather the other blind men to discuss the extraterrestrial elephant in the room.

(EARLY DECEMBER...)

I'd gotten my mother to invite Leah and me over on Sunday, and Danny, Rachel, and the twins as well. Danny had grumbled at first about missing the football game, but I told him I was sure no one would mind if we had the broadcast on in the background. We compromised and agreed that we'd all get together after halftime.

Once we convened, we were, for better or worse, stuck inside, inasmuch as it was very, very cold out that afternoon. The women disappeared into the kitchen. My brother made himself comfortable on the living room couch, with the radio on. I was happy to entertain Abe and Bea in the spare bedroom—what used to be the bedroom I shared with Danny. In fact, our bunk beds were still in there. The twins and I, their "Uncle Jay," climbed up and onto the top bunk, which had been Danny's, of course.

"When your dad and I were kids," I told them, "in this very room, when the weather was lousy and we couldn't go outside... or if one of us was sick... or if it was just nighttime and we weren't ready to go to sleep, we used to play a game. We called it taking an alphabet journey. We'd pick a subject, a type of thing—like famous people or desserts or places we wanted to visit one day—and we'd try to come up with one for every letter of the alphabet. Does that make sense?"

Both twins nodded.

"Should we take an alphabet journey now?"

"Yes," said both Abe and Bea.

"Great," I said. "What should we think of?"

"Flowers!" Bea suggested.

"Sure," I said, not at all sure that I could name a flower for every letter of the alphabet, or even more than six or seven in total.

"Superheroes!" Abe countered.

"Also good. Let's do both," I told them, "like this: For each letter, you'll say the name of a flower, Bea, and Abe will say the name of a superhero. Got it?"

"Got it," they said.

"And I'll name a... phobia."

"A what?"

"A phobia is an extreme, often irrational fear of something. I'll name things that some people are really, really scared of. Here we go... A."

Of course I'm not going to recount all twenty-five superheroes, flowers, and phobias that Abe, Bea, and I named—or made up and hoped the other two wouldn't challenge—over the next half hour or so. When that game ended, we found other things to do, and I enjoyed spending that time with the twins, as I always did. Being an uncle wasn't at all the same as being a father, I knew, but I believed that if I ever had kids half as sweet as my brother's, I would find it rewarding.

I popped out of the bedroom into the living room to ask my brother if the game was over yet.

"No," he said, "but soon. Unfortunately."

"What's the score?" I asked.

"28–21," Danny said.

"Who's winning?"

"28."

"Hilarious," I said.

"Washington," Danny said. "And it looks like it's going to stay that way."

I returned to the bedroom.

"Guys," I said to Abe and Bea, "why don't you go see what your mom and grandma and Leah are up to? I bet they'd like a visit. Maybe there's even a treat in the kitchen."

"Okay," they said and left. When they were gone, I closed the bedroom door behind them and went to the closet for a box I'd secreted there a couple of days earlier. In the box was what I'd need to bring my practical joke to fruition that afternoon. I first consulted my schedule for the appropriate entry, found the number of the associated envelope, extracted that envelope from the box, then replaced the box in the closet. I'd have to return another time to destroy the remainder of the contents, but for the time being it could all just stay out of sight. The last thing I did was erase the penciled number from the reverse of the envelope before emerging once more from the bedroom.

Danny was not in the living room, so I surmised that the football game had in fact ended. I found everyone in the kitchen.

"So?" I said to my brother. "It's over?"

"It's over."

"28–21 Washington?"

Danny nodded. He had pushed a piece of honey cake into his mouth.

"That's so weird," I told Danny. "Because early this week, I had a dream about a football game. At the Polo Grounds. And I could see the teams clearly: the Giants and the Redskins. Even stranger, I could see the scoreboard in my dream, too. And I thought, wouldn't it be amazing if the actual game turned out the way it did in my dream?"

"So," I continued, "I got out of bed and typed up the final score of the game—the game in my dream—onto a note card. And then, just to prove that I'd had this dream before today, you know what I did?"

"What did you do?" Leah asked.

"Oh," I said, "I didn't realize you were listening." But of course I'd realized it. I needed the others to be listening so that Danny would look stupid.

"I put the note in an envelope and mailed it to myself."

"You don't say," Leah said.

"And I brought the envelope here with me." I withdrew it from my pocket and offered it to my brother. "Would you open it, Danny?"

Danny seemed confused, but he took the sealed envelope from me all the same.

"You mailed this to yourself?" he asked.

"Yes," I said. "See the postmark?"

Danny looked. "December 8, 1948," he read. "You want me to open it?"

"Please." I was becoming concerned that my practical joke was going to go right over my brother's head.

Danny tore open the envelope and pulled out the index card.

"Washington: 28, New York: 21," he read. "Holy crap!"

"Dunny!" my mother admonished. The twins giggled.

"But Ma!" Danny said, excited. "Germy predicted the score of the Giants game! Not just who would win, but the actual score! He saw it in a dream!" *Okay,* I thought. *He's taken the bait.*

"You did that, Jeremiah?" My mother had not been paying me her full attention, I gathered. That was okay, though.

"I did," I told her.

"Germy," Danny said, "you could have made money!" *Hook, line, and stinker.*

"Yes, Jeremiah. You could have made a lot of money." This was Leah speaking, to my surprise. She seemed to be smirking when she said it.

"Well," I said. "I... it was a dream. I wasn't going to bet money based on a dream."

"Do you think it'll happen again?" Danny asked.

"Danny," Rachel said, "you might have a gift."

"I want a gift!" Abe said. "Me too!" said Bea. "Chanukah's coming," my mother told them. "You'll get gifts then."

"My great aunt Minna had visions," Rachel went on. She turned to my mother and asked, "Is there a history of visions in your family?"

"Not that I know of," my mother admitted, "but maybe Jeremiah is the first. Wouldn't that be something? A man with one good eye having visions!"

And then, all of a sudden, I was worrying that my mother and my sister-in-law were genuinely considering the possibility that I might be clairvoyant, while my older brother, genius that he was, was imagining putting my gift to use at the bookmakers'.

"Kind of incredible, no?" I asked Leah, curious to know what she thought.

Again with the smirk.

"What?" I asked.

Leah looked to my mother, then to my brother, then to my brother's wife. They were all looking at me, perhaps waiting for me to say something profound. But instead Leah spoke.

"You do know how Jeremiah did this," she asked, "don't you? I mean, you don't believe that the score of a football game came to him in a dream, right?"

"Of course we believe him," my mother said. "Why wouldn't we believe him?"

"And the postmark proves it!" Danny added.

"He couldn't have mailed that card to himself today," Rachel said. "He was here the whole time."

I thought I saw Leah stifle a sigh.

"No, he didn't mail himself anything today. He mailed this card to himself on Monday, just as the postmark says. But he didn't mail himself just this card. He probably mailed himself... what, fifty cards? A hundred?"

"A *hundred* cards?" my mother asked. I knew she was at least partly thinking of the expense. She'd lived through the Depression. She saved broken rubber bands.

"One for each possible final score of the game," Leah explained. "Or... if not every possible score, then the most likely ones. And then he just needed to know which score was in which envelope, so he could produce the right one—as if it were the *only* one—when the actual game was over, today. In fact... Danny, can I see the envelope, please?"

Danny passed the envelope to Leah, who scrutinized it.

"Sneaky," she said, to me. "You numbered each one in pencil so you could erase the number. What number is this one? Fifty... six?"

"Fifty-six," I confirmed, not caring at all that she'd just exposed my trick. "You're wonderful," I told her, and I meant it.

"But, your dream—!" Danny exclaimed.

"Would you all wait here for a minute?" I asked my family. "I just want to get something."

I returned to my old bedroom for a box, which I then brought back to the kitchen. It wasn't the box with the other envelopes, though. It was a small black felt box.

"Leah," I said, then got down on one knee before her and held out the felt box. My mother and Rachel gasped, in a good way.

"Leah Rosenbaum," I asked, "will you marry me?"

"Of course," she said, and everyone clapped for us.

Then Leah opened the felt box and gasped. "Oof!" she said. "Another practical joke?"

"Oh, right," I said. "That's not your ring. That's my mother's aunt's ring. It's hideous. But the diamond is a good one, so we can use that, in a much nicer ring. It'll save us money."

"Which we wouldn't need to do," Leah pointed out, "if you would just bet on football games like your brother suggested."

"Exactly," Danny said. I swatted him on the shoulder.

"I love you," I told Leah. "And I am very impressed."

"Let me help next time," Leah offered, whispering in my ear.

"Really?"

"Really. I like your brother—I do, honestly, and Rachel too, and your mother—but they just make it so... rewarding."

(NOW LATE DECEMBER FOR A BIT...)

When I'd returned to Area 50, I found that Bradford and Smith had evidently gone home for the night. At least, they weren't there. I really can't say whether they'd gone home.

I let myself into the Science Room and into the presence of the item that I'd been shown earlier, and which made no sense to me, and somehow not just because it was supposedly from somewhere other than Earth. I stared at the thing for a long time, but it didn't become any clearer to me how the shard of an extraterrestrial spacecraft hull could have on it, and unmistakably so, a string of letters from the Modern Roman alphabet, and in their midst the same "letter" I'd tried to help a pair of advertising men introduce—pretending to reintroduce it—into that alphabet. But there were the letters:

DEFGHI

And why there? I found myself wondering. *Why between G and I? Why not at the end of the alphabet? Or the beginning. Or nowhere at all?*

It looked like it belonged, I thought, but then I supposed that any additional foreign item placed into an established series could—maybe even *would*—eventually appear familiar there. Especially if one stared long enough. And was very tired. And had been drinking gin.

Gin, I thought. Without the interloper, the abbreviated markings on the shard would have ended with GI, properly adjacent as they are in both the alphabet and the spirit. Of course, in the alphabet they're followed by...

Huh. Smith had insisted that the shard was real—and old. He hadn't specified how old, but if the shard had not ended just where it did, and the alphabetic sequence had continued intact, then *I*—the person, not the letter—would have been able at least to say whether the shard predated the year 1640 or instead—

"Professor Carp?"

Someone had said my name, and I jumped, nearly out of my own skin. If I'd been holding the shard, I almost certainly would have dropped it. Of course, it was made of something sturdy—it had already survived crashing to Earth from outside our planet's atmosphere, so it would have been fine, but still. No one wants to be that person, the one who drops alien spaceship remains. I had a bad enough reputation among humorless humans as it was.

"I'm sorry, Professor," said a woman. "I didn't mean to startle you." It was the woman I'd seen earlier, the one who'd brought the shard to Smith so he could show it to me.

"No, no," I said, meaningfully. "Actually, I owe you an apology. I nearly barreled you down this afternoon. That was... rude of me." *Is "barrel down" what I mean?* I wondered. *Or do people only barrel down Niagara Falls? Did I mean "bowl over"? Get a hold of yourself, Carp!*

"No apology necessary," she said. "You were understandably upset. I told them that just... *showing* you the debris like that might not be the best way to proceed, but they didn't listen to me."

"So you know... who I am?"

"Of course I do, Professor."

"Well, then you have me at something of a disadvantage," I confessed, "because no one has introduced me to you yet."

"My name is Iris. Iris Lucas."

I winced inwardly at the dissonance, but outwardly extended my hand, which Iris Lucas shook. "And you're Smith's assistant?" I asked, putting my foot in my mouth.

"No," Iris said, taking back her hand. "I'm his colleague. And, for that matter, yours."

It was my turn to blush. "Ah," I said eloquently. "And what is your... pleasure?" I was not doing much to regain any ground, I knew.

"Archaeometallurgy."

"That's a thing?" I asked.

"As much as crypto-linguistics, yes. Maybe even more so," she added. "I've met others in my field."

I laughed at that. "But you're—"

"A woman?" Iris challenged.

Don't say "pretty." Do not say "pretty," Jeremiah. Whatever you say, make sure that "pretty" is not it.

"—so young, I was going to say," I said.

Iris looked me square in my good eye. "We're the same age, I'm guessing. I might even have a year or two on you."

"You think so, do you?" Before Iris could answer my rhetorical question, I asked a real one: "What's Smith's area of expertise? Bradford introduced him as a 'specialist.'"

"Smith specializes..." Iris began, "in everything, really."

"He's that good, is he? So the crack science team examining the first alien spaceship to crash on Earth consists of an old German Hans-of-all-disciplines and an archaeometallurgist in her early thirties?"

"No," Iris said. "There's also an astrobiologist. Silas Sanderson. You won't enjoy meeting him."

"Why not?"

"Because he doesn't like you."

"How do you know that? Why do you know that?"

"He's mentioned it more than once. He was vehemently opposed to bringing you onto the team. He threatened to leave if Bradford approached you, in fact."

I didn't know what to say to that. Iris saw.

"The good news," she said, "is that he's in the desert in New Mexico, collecting samples, so you won't have to meet him for another couple of days."

"Maybe I can make my contribution before he gets back," I said.

"I can't imagine it'll take that long," Iris said. I could tell that she was teasing me, but I was thinking the very same thing in earnest. "I'm going home, Professor. Lock up when you're done?"

"Of course," I said. "It was very nice to meet you, Iris Lucas."

Don't tell her she smells good.

Don't say you like how her hair looks.

Do not compliment her on any part of her gross anatomy.

"Was there something else, Professor?"

"Nope," I said. "Have a good night."

Incredibly, I found myself thinking that spending more time with the alien spaceship shard might actually steady my nerves right then, but ultimately I decided just to leave Area 50.

The following morning, I didn't know quite how to proceed. That is, I had decided to join the secret special superteam, such as it was, and help however I could, but no one had told me *specifically* how to help, or even when. Or where, for that matter. We simply hadn't gotten to the logistics, so I didn't know whether I was expected to work regular hours on site—9 a.m. to 5 p.m., Monday through Friday, for instance, with an hour off for lunch each day—or just to be available to consult as needed, or something in between, such as dropping by Area 50 from time to time. I figured that I wouldn't return to the Museum before speaking to Bradford by phone again, but I didn't want to call him too early in the day, so I decided to make myself breakfast at home and play things by ear.

I was *just* sitting down to a plate of scrambled eggs and some toast with coffee when there was a no-nonsense knock on the door to my apartment, which I opened to find five very serious-looking men, all dressed in dark suits, in standard two-in-front, three-behind formation. Before I could even ask them what they wanted or whether they all shopped at the same store, they were in my apartment, three of them searching it, leaving nothing unmolested.

"Hey!" I protested feebly.

"Professor Carp," said one of the two men who wasn't ransacking my home, "please come with us."

"Where?" I asked. "Why?" I asked.

"You are wanted for questioning in connection with the disappearance of government property," said the other man flanking me, leading me out of my apartment. Fortunately, I'd gotten dressed—eyepatch and all—before making my breakfast, which, unfortunately, it looked like I wasn't going to get to eat.

"I don't understand," I told them. "What government property?"

But neither man answered me.

"Am I supposed to know what you're talking about?"

Again, silence. The next thing I knew, I was being shepherded by the two non-ransackers into the back seat of a nondescript automobile double-parked outside my building. There were already two other men in the front seat.

"I want to make a phone call," I said as the vehicle pulled into traffic. It was a silly thing to say, really, from the back seat of a car. Yet I continued: "I want to speak to Agent... Bradford. I don't know his first name. He might not have one. But he's with the government."

The man in the passenger seat turned to face me and said, "And I want to speak to you, Carp."

"Bradford! What is this? What's going on?"

"I'll ask the questions, Carp," Bradford said. "But not yet," he added. "Just sit back and enjoy the ride. We'll be at the department office soon, and then we'll have a nice private chat."

Ah. I understood. I really did. I kept quiet. Bradford had just telegraphed something very important to me. *He* wasn't able to speak freely in the car. I would just have to wait until we reached the office of his department—whichever "department" that was; Bradford hadn't told me that, either, I realized.

As it happened, we weren't driving for very long at all, but in that time I managed to do some analytical thinking and arrive at some comforting conclusions: Bradford's presence suggested strongly that whatever had occurred was related to Area 50. And if something had disappeared from Area 50—something I was supposed to have taken, or helped go missing—then it had to be something I knew about and which I would want to steal or help steal. What I knew about in Area 50 was more or less limited to what I'd been shown—the hull shard with the aitch, specifically—and what I'd noticed, which was a lot of science equipment. None of the equipment was of any use to me personally, and although it was entirely possible that I could have stolen some or all of it to fence it, that just seemed very unlikely. How much would a plasmogrometer, or what have you, bring on the black market, anyway? Was there even a black market for laboratory equipment? I did not know. That's the sort of thing I prefer not to know.

That left the shard itself, which of course was at once priceless and worthless, at least in this context. It was priceless as evidence that Earth was not the only planet in the Universe inhabited by intelligent life, among other things. It was worthless as a collectible, other than to someone willing to keep it completely out of sight and never to let on that he owned it, for fear that it would be the target of the next person who wanted to own it in total secrecy and was likewise willing to obtain it unlawfully, and so on. While some unscrupulous collector of extraterrestrial curiosities might have made it worth my while to abscond with the shard and turn it over, I'd only been made aware of its existence the day before. Who could have gotten to me so quickly? No one, really.

The most likely scenario, then, was that I'd absconded with the shard for my own nefarious reasons—which of course I didn't have—in which case it would be in my apartment, where Bradford's men would find it, or hidden somewhere else, except that it wasn't, and Bradford knew this. Because Bradford knew that not only did I have no reason to hide the shard, but to the contrary, every reason to make it public. The shard represented something unique for me, inasmuch as it could have vindicated me and removed the stain the hoax had left on my reputation... but, then again, it didn't. Because I'd sworn up and down— on the record of a Congressional committee hearing—that the hoax was just that, with no basis in fact and invented as a harmless lark. To change my tune and claim that I'd been right all along about the existence of the aitch—as proven by alien spaceship debris—would not have helped my cause. It would have just done more damage. So I had neither reason to keep the shard under wraps nor to make it known to the world.

In short, I had no reason to steal the shard from Area 50, and I knew that Bradford knew this.

Why then had he interrupted my near-breakfast to question me when he could have just called me and told me to pursue my work on the project from home? Did he know I was having eggs again, and was he just trying to limit my fat intake? That was probably also not the reason, I thought.

Having done all the thinking I could think and reached all the conclusions I could reach, I thought I'd make some conversation.

"Driver, this is a very nice car. Custom-made? Bulletproof?"

The driver didn't answer me. Bradford said nothing either.

"Speaking of cars, have you guys heard that story about Henry Ford? That when he interviewed potential executives, he'd sit down to a small meal with the candidate? If the other man put salt on his food before tasting it, Ford would disqualify him from consideration? Because it showed, to Ford's mind, that the other man made arbitrary decisions based on habit, not reasoned decisions based on observation and analysis?"

No response.

"Well," I continued, "even though it sounds pretty good, it's almost certainly not true. But you know what is true about Henry Ford? He did *not* like Jews. He even won an award from Nazi Germany for his anti-Semitism. Can you imagine? Is this car a Ford? It's pretty comfortable, I have to admit, but I still wouldn't buy one."

Nothing from the front seat.

"Are we there yet?" I asked.

But I wasn't really inclined to be annoying just for the sake of being annoying, especially after determining that I was not actually in trouble with the government and that Bradford was keeping silent only because he had to, for reasons I had to presume he would reveal to me later. So for the remainder of the car ride, I looked out my window.

The sidewalks of New York City were, as they always were, crowded, full of men, women, and children—humans, probably, none of them aware that our planet had been visited, possibly more than once, by aliens, and no doubt happier not to know as much. I'd been happier not to know, I thought.

But, really, had I? Learning the new truth had put my life to that point into a very different perspective, I had to admit. In a much larger Universe, my mistakes and missteps were a lot less significant. And that was oddly comforting.

"Carp," Bradford said, finally, bringing me abruptly back to Earth. "We're here."

"I didn't take the shard," I told Bradford, "and I have no idea who did."

Bradford's eyebrow rose. Just one, though. The right one. My right, his left. Bradford's left eyebrow rose. Bradford raised his left eyebrow, then said: "No one said anything about the shard being missing."

"No one had to," I countered, leaving my own eyebrows where they were. "I worked it all out during the ride here."

Here, in that context, was an office we'd made our way to, just Bradford and I, once the driver of the car I'd been placed into had pulled up to a building I would never be able to pick out of a lineup. It was a nicely enough appointed office, but there was nothing to indicate that it was Bradford's office, specifically. On the wall, for example, was a framed photograph of the President, but on the desk were no pictures of anyone's wife or kids. It might have been a multipurpose government agent office shared by whoever needed it on any given day. To my great pleasure, however, there was a hot cup of coffee and an onion bagel with cream cheese and lox waiting for me when we arrived.

"The shard is gone," I continued between bites and sips. "And I was the last one at the museum last night. So naturally I'm a suspect. But I'm not your man," I insisted.

"I know," Bradford said. "And you're correct, of course: The shard is missing. Smith was first to Area 50 this morning. He called me immediately."

"But—" I tried to interrupt. Bradford didn't allow it.

"You had your say," he said. "Now let me finish. You were the last to leave, but you're not a suspect. Still, the fact that the shard was removed after you were shown Area 50—and only after that—isn't a coincidence."

"But isn't it, though?"

"I think I once told you that I don't believe in coincidences," Bradford said.

"That was yesterday, Bradford," I reminded him. "We only met yesterday. We've known each other for less than 24 hours. Of course, you were following me for a little while before that."

"Yes, well..."

Even though he and I had just met, I felt sure that Bradford's comment was unusual. "Go on," I said.

Bradford winced, almost imperceptibly. "It now seems likely," he admitted with no small amount of difficulty and what might have been humility, "that I wasn't the only one following you."

"I'm sorry?"

"The theft of a top secret item from a top secret location at the first opportunity after you were brought on board a top secret project team tells me that someone else, someone other than me, was watching you, waiting for you to be let in on the secrets."

"But why me?" I asked. "Why would anyone imagine that I would *ever* be let in on those secrets?"

"For the very reason that you *were*. Because of what you knew—or pretended to know—about Glyph Two-Six. But this other person didn't know, or didn't believe, that you'd made up what you made up. Or didn't care either way, as long as we— as long as I—revealed to you where we were keeping the thing. From space."

"But"—and I realized that I was starting a lot of sentences this way—"the thing from space, as you say, isn't worth anything to anyone, other than as material to examine, as far as I understand. And it's not the kind of thing that anyone could keep hidden for very long, anyway—again, I imagine. So, really, the only reason I can think of—the only practical reason— for stealing the shard would be to keep you... us... Smith and company, anyway—from examining it further. Yet short of destroying the remnant, which I suppose is something someone could do, there's nowhere on Earth the thief, or thieves, could take it where we… or you… or your secret agent subordinates… wouldn't eventually find it."

I stopped talking. Bradford didn't say anything right away, so I thought about what I'd just said. And I think that's what Bradford wanted me to do. Because I suspect that he didn't want to be the one to say what had to be said next.

"Wait," I said, because I also didn't want to give voice to such an outlandish—and, frankly, terrifying—notion. "You don't really think…" I couldn't quite get the words out, so I backed up and took a running leap at it.

"You don't really think they're here, do you? Aliens? For their spaceship piece?"

"It's a possibility we have to consider," Bradford said. "We know that they can get here."

"So you think… an alien was following me? An extraterrestrial was keeping tabs on me?" I shuddered.

"Possibly."

"And I led him—"

"Or them," Bradford interjected, only increasing the amplitude of my shudders.

"—right to Area 50 and the shard, which now might be on its way back to outer space?"

"Don't blame yourself, Carp. You couldn't have known."

"I'm not blaming myself, Bradford! What? Why would you even…?"

There was a knock at the door, and a young government lackey popped his head in to ask if we needed more coffee. Bradford said that he did not. I said that I did, that I needed a *lot* more coffee.

"So… why did you bring me here, Bradford? Why didn't you just call me this morning and tell me that the project's off and I should just go about my business and pretend I'd never heard of you or Area 50? Why did you have to pretend to arrest me? And why did your men have to turn my apartment upside down?"

"Carp," Bradford said, "my men turned your apartment upside down just to be sure the spaceship piece isn't there. I pretended to arrest you so that other men of mine could watch for anyone who might still be trailing you. And I didn't call you to tell you that the project is off because the project is still very much on. Your part of it, anyway. Smith and the others are going to have some downtime, but you don't need the actual shard to do your part. You didn't need it to pretend to have found evidence of Glyph Two-Six in the history of human civilization and written communication. You shouldn't need the shard to actually find evidence of your aitch now."

"Aw," I said. "You used my name for it. That means a lot to me."

"Carp," Bradford said, "please go to a library or something."

"There's one on Fifth Avenue," I said. "And it's supposed to be pretty big."

Before heading to the library, I returned to my apartment. I'd expected to find it in complete disarray. I was surprised. If Bradford's men had turned my living quarters upside-down, they'd turned it fully right-side-up again before clearing out. And they'd cleaned it, too. They'd swept. They'd vacuumed. They'd washed, dried, and put away the dishes that had been in my sink (and discarded my scrambled eggs, apparently). They'd taken out my trash. They'd replaced a bulb in a lamp in my living room that had been literally on the blink. There was no dust anywhere, and the whole place smelled better than it had in a while.

If I'd known that participating in an abortive hoax on the American public, ignoring the advice of counsel and giving testimony to a Congressional subcommittee, getting fired from my tenure-track academic position, losing my fiancée, being recruited by a secret government task force, and learning that Earth had been visited by aliens would lead to my coming home to an apartment that clean... no, of course I would not have chosen to do it all again the very same way. That would be ridiculous. But the place really did look terrific.

I went to my desk for the journal I liked to have with me when doing research. On my desk, next to my journal, was a collection of scraps of paper that I surmised the government agents/cleaners had not known where to file but had not wanted to discard lest they be important. After all, who knew how a crypto-linguistic genius like me organized his thoughts and notes.

I spread the scraps out, and one in particular caught my eye. I immediately wished that the G-Men had destroyed that one. Indeed, I wished I had never seen it in the first place.

The previous week, when I'd visited my office at the college, an odd thing had happened, something I probably should have wondered more about at the time. Of course, realizing as much after the fact isn't very helpful at all. But they say that hindsight is 20/20, and that's true even for a man with only one good eye.

Even though Gil Silver was the only other person I'd seen there, someone else must have been around, and looking for me, no less, but it seemed that we'd managed to miss each other. When I'd first arrived, I'd checked my mail in the department office. There was nothing pressing, but I'd taken the papers from my pigeonhole to my office, where I deposited them on my desk and forgot about them. But later, when I was leaving the building again, I forgot that I had already checked my mail. So I checked my mailbox again. It should have been empty, but it wasn't.

I found a slip of paper that I'm certain had not been there earlier. On the slip of paper was a note, to the effect that someone had stopped by to have a word with me. There was a number as well, and a request that I call the number, at my convenience. Which I did, when I got home. I spoke with a pleasant, if somewhat robotic, woman who identified herself as the head secretary of an advertising agency. Her bosses—two of them—were the ones who wanted the actual word with me. But she couldn't tell me anything else. Admittedly intrigued, and having very little else on my calendar, I made arrangements to meet with the men in my office at the college the following day.

If I had to pinpoint when everything that had gone wrong had started to go wrong, it would likely be that meeting.

(RETURNING TO EARLY DECEMBER...)

I had barely gotten comfortable in my office chair when I looked up to see that my company had arrived, quite silently.

"Professor," said the man on my left, extending a hand to me. "My name is Allan—two a's, two l's—Little, and this is my partner, Alan Green."

"Two a's, one l," the man on the right said, offering me his hand to shake in turn. "We're in advertising, I think our secretary mentioned. We have our own firm: Little, Green. You've probably never heard of it, or us."

"I have never, indeed," I confirmed. Before the meeting, I had pulled a couple of chairs into my office from elsewhere, and I invited the men to be seated.

"You've almost certainly bought something or other from one or more of our clients, though," Little said with a chuckle, as he sat. "And that's how we know we're doing our job well."

"But we didn't come to sell you anything," Green assured me. "Actually, we're here to ask if you'd be willing to work with us."

"I'm flattered," I said, "but I have a job. A career, in fact, one that I like very much. I'm not looking to make a change."

"Oh, we have no illusions of luring you away from academia, Professor," Green said. "To the contrary, your academic credentials are what we'd be looking to leverage."

"To what end?" I asked. "My academic credentials are, generally speaking, not for anyone but me to leverage."

"We appreciate that," Green said. "But we figured it wouldn't hurt to ask for your help."

"We need to sell the public on a concept," Little began to explain, "before our clients can sell them new goods and services. If our concept is to be convincing, though… *compelling,* then it can't come from us, or even from one of our accounts. It has to come from an authority. The right kind of authority, I mean."

"Can you get a bit more specific, guys?" I asked. I couldn't deny that my interest was piqued, and I really did want to know more.

"Sure," said Green (though I admit that I was having trouble remembering which was who. They kind of looked alike, I realized). "We need to add a letter to the alphabet."

"I'm sorry?"

"Letters sell," Little asserted. "Vowels, specifically. But American marketers have run through them very quickly. The useful ones, anyway. And there weren't many to begin with."

"You… you've lost me," I confessed.

"Let's take a step back," Green said, "three years back. Since the end of the war, things have been looking up all over, but here in America especially. Times, Professor Carp, are good. For most people, anyway. Most people have money to spend. And, in any event, it's the people with money to spend who we're interested in, of course. The goal, as always, is to get the moneyed people's money."

"It's not a complicated system, really," Little put in.

"I guess not," I said.

"As far as marketing goes, once peace was declared, it was back to basics. Emphasis on the classics," Green said.

"The A-frame house," Little noted. "The A-line dress."

"Sturdy, hardworking, uncomplicated mainstays that gave the people comfort," Green continued. "But the war was ended with the A-bomb, so there was an almost immediate push to move to a new letter."

Little took over: "Rather than go to B, though, we went straight to E, another vowel, with its connotations of e-lectricity, which had been the last thing, before atomic implosion, to revolutionize the world. So we were selling new e-quipment of every shape and size and color. Everything imaginable was re-branded with an e-prefix, or 'e-fix,' in brandspeak—restaurants with actual cooks were replaced by 'e-teries' with automated carousels; iceboxes were chucked in favor of 'e-frigerators'; even charities, which don't plug into an outlet, jumped on the bandwagon and became 'e-leemosynary institutions.'"

"But soon enough the bloom was off that rose as well," Green resumed, "and we moved on, as a country of consumers, to I. The appeal of the *i-* opener was that it personalized things. It made the consumer feel an intimate personal connection with each i-tem. Of course, the most famous of these was the iRon, which—ironically, you might say—was an electrical version of a steam-powered contrivance."

"O is a non-starter," Little lamented. "It makes everything sound like a prayer or a plea. 'Oh, no!' 'Oh, Lord!' And U does just the opposite of I—it leaves the u-ser feeling lazy and demanding."

"We managed to blow through the three useful vowels in record time," Green groused, "and the other two aren't viable."

"And Y?" I asked.

"Y, indeed. That's exactly right," Little answered. "We won't even try it. Starting a product name with a Y would have consumers asking, literally, *why* they should bother. Y could never be used. No, the industry needs an all-new, all-purpose vowel."

"But it can't just be invented, of course," Green said, "or it will have no cachet. It has to... have existed. It has to be unearthed, discovered. It has to have a pedigree. And so it has to be found by an authority."

"We need—the business of America needs," Little wrapped up their spiel, "a new vowel, and we want you to bring it to life. Or back to life, if you will. Give it a name, a history. And a reason for being returned to the alphabet."

Allan and Alan said no more.

After a moment, as politely as I could manage, I said: "Gentlemen, that's insane. It would possibly be more amusing than anything else I've ever done, but still insane. You're talking about perpetrating a hoax," I said. "You know that, I'm sure."

"But a harmless one," Little said, even though it might have been Green's turn to speak.

"We'll reveal that it was a publicity stunt as soon as the letter gains traction," Green said. "Sooner, if it doesn't."

"How would you spread the word, though? Of my... discovery, I mean. Am I supposed to issue a press release? I don't think I could get the college involved," I told them.

"Well, how would you announce an actual discovery of an actual lost letter?"

"I'd publish a paper," I said. "In a journal."

"Then do that."

"One doesn't just 'do that,' though," I explained. "Like vowels, there are only a handful of journals where such a paper would be appropriate, and those journals have professional, circumspect editors who don't just print whatever they receive, even if it comes from someone they should be able to trust. Academic papers are reviewed, sources are checked, research is verified..."

"Okay, Professor," Little said. "Okay. We get the picture. You know the ropes much better than we do. That's why we came to you. Let us figure out how to spread the word—"

"The letter," Green said, clearly pleased with himself.

"—the letter," Little agreed, "while you work on the letter itself. How about that?"

Hmm. I'd be lying if I said it didn't sound like a lot of fun, what these men were proposing. I enjoyed crypto-linguistics very much, but opportunities for lightheartedness were few and far between. For instance, it had been some five years since I'd floated the notion that Q and R were supposed to represent O and P without their pants on...

"I get to name it?"

The men nodded as one.

"Would I be deciding what it looks like?"

"It's being designed by other experts as we speak," Little said. "Everything else about it, though, is yours to fashion as you see fit."

I looked from one man to the other then back again. They looked like men I could trust. And they were offering me an absurdly exciting opportunity to be a part of a preposterously diverting lark. I certainly *wanted* to participate...

"Let me think about it," I said.

"Of course," Little agreed, shaking my hand again. "We'll get a dossier to you as soon as possible. And a check, too. For the consultation."

"Wait," I said. "I don't think I can let you pay me."

"No?" Green asked

"Probably not," I said.

"Well, that hardly seems fair," Little remarked.

"I appreciate that you didn't come here today to ask for free work," I told the men, "but taking money on top of helping with a hoax might be something I'd have a hard time justifying. You know, compared to just helping with a hoax out of the goodness of my heart. So maybe let's just table discussion of compensation."

"We understand, Professor," Green said. "For now, the good job we have every confidence you would do will have to be its own reward."

"For now," Little echoed. "And we would indeed encourage you to have fun with it! We'll look forward to hearing from you soon, Doctor Carp."

"We're quite confident that you're the right man for this mission," Alan flattered me.

And I probably was. Who better than Dr. Jeremiah Carp to discover a "lost" letter of the alphabet? Who else would leap at the chance to convince the world that we needed another vowel—and then to pull it out of his sleeve just when we needed it most?

(BACK ONCE MORE TO LATE DECEMBER...)

The American Museum of Natural History is one of the most impressive of many institutions situated on Manhattan Island. Without question, the Main Branch of the New York Public Library is another.

The flagship building of the city's library system, and a historic landmark, at Fifth Avenue and 42nd Street, the Main Branch is perhaps best known for its Main Reading Room, a majestic space with 52-foot-high ceilings lit by massive windows and grand chandeliers, furnished with sturdy wood tables, comfortable chairs, and brass lamps, and lined with thousands of reference works on open shelves along the floor level and a balcony. Over the years, I had done no small amount of research and writing at the Library, and I relished every opportunity I had to visit the place, professionally or otherwise. I was genuinely looking forward to spending time there again, looking for evidence of the existence of the aitch in, well, anywhere I could find it.

I won't bore you, or myself, describing the two full days I spent pawing through and poring over hundreds of various volumes spanning multiple centuries, many of which I had to request from the stacks on the lower floors, and some of which I was permitted to peruse only in private chambers, wearing cotton gloves, in the presence of a staff archivist, only to come up with nothing to show for my efforts but eye strain.

In fact, I had to insist that I be allowed to see some items, even after verifying my academic credentials (I didn't have anything to prove my new quasi-governmental credentials). The Gutenberg Bible, for one. To be completely honest, I hadn't known going in that the New York Public Library has a Gutenberg *Biblia Latina* in its collection. Only in the course of my research on the first day did I discover as much, so I made it a point to try to examine it during the second day. When I asked, however, I met with some resistance.

"May I see it?" I asked a librarian of the Rare Book Division.

"May I ask why you wish to see it, sir?" he asked me.

"I am researching the existence, or non-existence, of a letter of the alphabet," I said.

"Which alphabet?"

"The Roman alphabet."

"Ancient or Modern?"

"First one," I said, "then the other."

"Indeed," the librarian sniffed. "Even so, I doubt that the Biblia Latina will be of use to you."

"Because?" I challenged the man.

"Because the significance of the work is not readily appreciated," he said, then added, "by all."

"Well," I said, "one doesn't need a doctorate in crypto-linguistics, which I have, to perceive that you're not quite saying what you mean. But I think I'm catching on. You suppose that I lack a certain... capacity, let's call it, to perceive the merits and charms of the first substantial printed book of Western Civilization, arguably the greatest human achievement of the second millennium."

The librarian did not agree with me, but neither did he disagree with me. What he said was, "There are many other noteworthy volumes in the library's extensive collection that you might find more compatible with your, shall we say, point of view."

"My point of view," I repeated. "You do realize that without the point of view of my people, there would be no Bible, right?"

"I beg your pardon, sir? Your people?

"Jews," I said. "Most of that book is about *my* ancestors."

"Sir," the librarian said, lowering his voice. "I was not implying that you should not examine the Bible because of your faith."

"No?" And here I had been ready to give the man a piece of my Semitic mind.

"No," he assured me. "I was trying to convey that I don't think the Bible will be as impressive to a man with impaired vision."

"So... it's not *Jew*," I said, "it's *eye?*"

"You can put it that way," he said.

"Come on," I said. "Show me the damned book."

But not even the *Biblia Latina*—or any of the other rare books I also manhandled—shed any light, and at the end of my second day of fruitless exertion, I departed the Library and bid farewell to the stone lions out front, Patience and Fortitude. I had no more of either. And I would have to report my failure to Bradford.

Of course, it wasn't my fault that I couldn't find anything. That was the whole mystery, after all. The letter had been erased from history—somehow, somewhen—but thoroughly. And, come to think of it, wasn't it the complete lack of evidence that the aitch had ever been—just *been*—that had been my undoing? (Yes. It had.) Wasn't that what the renowned alphabetologist Vincent Guilmard had recently spent an hour testifying to, just to impeach my character unnecessarily, prompting me to admit under oath, in no uncertain terms, and against the advice of counsel, that I had not ever believed that there had at any time been a twenty-sixth letter in the Modern Roman alphabet? Yes. It was.

Guilmard had recounted in nearly unendurable detail the research he had done to support his refutation of my assertion (which, of course was never my assertion). Guilmard had explained persuasively that there existed not a scintilla of evidence of the existence of the aitch. Guilmard had made plain that the aitch was a figment of my imagination. If Guilmard had not been able to uncover anything, then how would I?

Except that, as it turned out, the aitch *had* existed. According to the aliens.

Which meant that Guilmard had possibly missed something. Or Guilmard was keeping something covered up.

Either way, I wanted to speak to him. That is, I really did not want to speak with him, but I figured I had to.

If I was going to speak to Guilmard about the aitch, though, and if I was going to have a productive conversation with him, I would have to let him in on the Big Secret. I couldn't let someone else in on the Big Secret without permission, however. So I would have to speak to Bradford about speaking to Guilmard.

Back in my apartment, I thought about how nice it would be not to have to talk to anybody about anything. Then, with a sigh, I called Bradford.

"I need to talk to Vincent Guilmard," I said. I knew I wouldn't need to remind Bradford who Guilmard was.

"About Glyph Two-Six?"

"Not about the weather."

"I suppose you can do that," Bradford said.

"But I'll need to tell him about the shard," I said.

"You can't do that," Bradford told me.

"Bradford," I explained, "talking to Guilmard about the letter without talking about the rest isn't going to get me anywhere. I appreciate the need for secrecy, but if I'm going to get anywhere with this, I need to pick the brain of someone who might actually know something about it. And I suspect Guilmard knows more than he let on in Washington."

Bradford was silent for a moment.

I sighed again. "You think so, too," I said. "Don't you?"

Bradford said: "The thought has crossed my mind."

"Then look," I suggested. "Guilmard doesn't know that I've been made privy to anything. Guilmard probably thinks I'm a crackpot. At best, he thinks I'm a petty con artist. That'll work to our advantage. Anything I tell him can be denied as the ravings of a nut job. And he might figure that he can speak freely to me, since I've been wholly discredited and no one's going to take me seriously anymore."

Bradford thought about this. Then he said, "All right. You can talk to Guilmard. You can tell him about the shard. Just don't be too convincing."

"I'll do my best," I promised. "Oh, and Bradford, can you get me his number?"

I didn't know when I'd be able to call Guilmard—and I assumed that he'd returned to England, so I would have to take the time difference into account when scheduling our conversation—but that didn't stop me from anticipating how excruciatingly awkward the exchange would be.

Professor Guilmard, this is Jeremiah Carp. Remember me? You made me look like a complete fool in front of members of my country's legislature for no good reason. Yes, that Jeremiah Carp. Listen, do you have a few minutes to talk about aliens visiting Earth?

My phone rang and I jumped out of my chair, nearly spilling the drink I'd poured myself after speaking with Bradford.

"Hello?"

"You can speak to Guilmard tomorrow morning." It was Bradford again. "I had it arranged. You can call him from a secure line at Area 50."

"Thanks, Bradford," I said.

"Just try to keep it brief," Bradford requested. "Long-distance calls aren't cheap."

"You're a true patriot, Bradford," I said. "I'll see you at the museum in the morning."

(EARLY DECEMBER...)

After spending a very pleasant afternoon with Leah—we'd had sandwiches at a place called Agnes' Deli and then caught a showing of *The Treasure of the Sierra Madre* (because nothing I said could get Leah to see *Adams and Caruso Meet the Loch Ness Monster*)—I returned home to find that a large manila envelope had been slid under the door to my apartment. I presumed it contained the letter dossier that Allan and Alan had told me to watch for—even though I didn't recall having given them my address. I tore open the envelope like it was a birthday present and I was turning 5, not 35.

When I got my first look at the contents, I wasn't disappointed, exactly, but I was surprised, even if I'm not sure why I was surprised. The "letter" Allan Little and Alan Green had commissioned and were planning to persuade the American public to add to their everyday alphabet was boring, plain and simple.

I hadn't been expecting something more complicated, necessarily, nor should I have been—none of the letters in the Modern Roman alphabet is, really—but this symbol was the epitome of simplicity, or nearly so: Three straight lines— two vertical strokes, connected at their midpoints by a single horizontal cross-stroke. And that was it. It looked like a capital A, actually, only pried apart at the apex so that the uprights were parallel. Or even just a capital I, of the variety with the top and bottom bars, but turned on its side and made a bit taller. No curves, in any event. Right angles only. Zero sex appeal, you might say.

Allan and Alan had commissioned this new letter, though. I had to believe that they'd done their homework, so to speak, before engaging a letter designer, and also that the designer they'd hired had in turn done his homework, presumably studying the existing letters of our alphabet and determining what makes them tick. Maybe when we were all on the other side of the big reveal, I'd be able to pick the brain of the designer and learn what his thought process had been in settling on two vertical lines and a horizontal one.

So as things stood, the public was not going to be wowed by this letter, I was certain. Not visually, anyway. People would not wonder where this letter had been all their lives. It was inoffensive, but it was also nothing to get excited about. It was not a letter the people *had to have* in their alphabet. Which meant that the people were going to have to be given not just good reason but unequivocal, undeniable reason to "reinstate" the letter. The masses would have to believe that not letting the letter back into the alphabet would be tantamount to shunning a starving orphan on Christmas Eve, or even to telling Mary and Joseph that there's no room at the inn. To leave this letter in the past, where it had languished for centuries, would be unthinkable, unforgivable, indefensible. It would, in short, be a crime against humanity—nay, worse: a sin!

At the very least, a *shanda*. A shame, in Yiddish. A scandal.

And of course, a scandal is exactly what everyone got.

(LATE DECEMBER...)

"Professor Guilmard," I began, "thank you for agreeing to speak with me. I trust you made it back home safely and soundly, hale and heartily... and all that, wot?"

I couldn't see him, but I knew that Bradford was standing behind my chair, and I could sense him regretting letting me make this phone call. Even though he'd arranged for a transmission that could not (easily) be intercepted, he could still be mortified by my end of the conversation. And I imagined that he was already.

Ah, but wasn't I supposed to come across as the odd, untrustworthy loon with the crazy notions? Wasn't that our angle?

"How may I help you, Mister Carp?"

Mister. That stung, but I let it pass. I knew I was still Doctor Carp. I'd lost my job, not my degree.

"Professor," I said, "I've been thinking a great deal about some of the things you said when we were in Washington."

"I imagine you have, young man."

"Yes, well, I've been wondering in particular about the approach you took to researching the existence of a lost letter of the alphabet—"

"There is no lost letter, Mister Carp."

"Of course not, Professor. Forgive me. I'm not trying to convince anyone otherwise. You might recall that I never was. Rather, I'm... I'm trying to improve my own research methods, and it occurred to me to ask how you would look for evidence of something no one believes ever existed. As opposed to confirming what everyone already believes," I added.

"Such as what, Mister Carp?"

"Such as, well, such as a lost letter of an alphabet."

Guilmard sighed in England, and I might have heard him in New York even if we had not been on a transatlantic telephone call. *There is no lost letter of the alphabet. Why must you carry on with this foolishness, sir? Are twenty-six letters not quite enough for you?*"

"I beg your pardon, Professor. Twenty-six?"

"What's that?"

"You asked if twenty-six letters weren't enough. But of course you meant to say 'twenty-five.'"

"Yes. Twenty-five. Of course."

"Because, of course, as every schoolchild knows, there are only twenty-five letters in the Modern Roman alphabet," I said, "just as there always have been."

"Precisely," Guilmard agreed. "Now, Professor Carp, it is growing late, so if there is nothing further..."

"I understand," I said. "You've been more than courteous, and I don't wish to take up any more of your time. Thank you. Good night."

And I hung up the phone in Area 50.

"You didn't get what you wanted," Bradford remarked, stepping into my view.

"I was never going to," I said.

"Meaning?"

"Meaning either Professor Vincent Guilmard isn't nearly as knowledgeable about relevant matters as were led to believe in Washington," I elaborated, "or that wasn't Guilmard. First, he slipped up and referred to a twenty-six-letter alphabet. Then he seemed unaware that for quite a while the Modern Roman alphabet had only twenty-three letters, suggesting that he's more familiar with the way things were on Earth a very long time ago than how they were merely a long time ago."

"Carp," Bradford said evenly, "you're suggesting that Guilmard... is an alien?"

"Or was replaced by one."

"Seriously?"

"I... I have no idea, Bradford. All I can say for sure—and you have no choice but to forgive me for saying this—is that the man I just spoke to does *not* know his ABCs. You might want to ring up British Intelligence."

"I'll take that under advisement," Bradford said, making it clear that he wasn't likely to do any such thing. "But meanwhile, what are you going to do next?"

"Me? What can I do? And what does it matter anyway?" I asked. "I mean, the shard is gone, and if it's gone where we suspect, then we're not getting it back. And if there ever was any historical evidence of Glyph Two-Six, we're unlikely to ever see that again either. These are some thorough extraterrestrials," I said. "So even if I could find our missing letter in the haystack of history, what would it get us? What good would it do humanity to know that we used to have another vowel? If we want a new vowel, we can just make one."

"Didn't you try that?"

"Sort of. Not exactly. Are you really asking, or just throwing that in my face?"

"I was reminding you why you were eager to help me when I first approached you. And that wasn't very long ago."

"Yes, well, I was. Sure. But now I'm just... I just don't see the point anymore. Someone wants us to stop trying."

"And that doesn't bother you, Carp? I wouldn't have taken you for the kind of man who goes away when someone asks you to. Just the opposite."

"Are you saying I'm annoying, Bradford?"

"I'm saying you're persistent, Carp, and persistence has its merits."

"I can bang my head against a wall with the best of them, Bradford, but I'm tired. I'm tired of having the rug pulled out from under me. My apartment is the cleanest it's ever been, but

I need to get the rest of my life back in order, and this doesn't seem to be the way to do that. I'm sorry. I have to go sort things out in the real world, in the present day."

Bradford extended his hand to me. "Thanks for your help, Professor. I'll let the others know you won't be returning."

Too bad I won't get to meet Silas Sanderson, I thought, but I didn't say as much aloud. "Take care, Bradford. Good luck with everything." I shook the man's hand, and then something occurred to me.

"Are you still going to have men watching me? Or, watching for... others watching me?"

"That probably isn't necessary any longer," Bradford said.

I squinted my good eye at him, but I still couldn't see what he was thinking, so I left it at that.

But something was nagging at me, and I didn't put my finger on it until I was good and soused at home, of course.

It doesn't add up, I thought, alternately fighting the gin and giving in to it. *The math doesn't work.*

But why was I thinking about numbers? Wasn't it letters that were the problem? Wasn't I drinking—more frequently, and just *more,* that week—in part to forget about letters? I really wasn't prepared to pick a fight with numbers too. There were just so many of them. *At least—at most?—there are only twenty-five letters,* I thought, just before I fell asleep on my couch in my clothes. At noon.

One of the most important lessons I learned from my father had to do with solving problems. Specifically, that the key to solving a problem is often in *defining* the problem. My father once told me of an afternoon when he was a boy and was returning home with vegetables from the market. His mother was waiting for the vegetables to prepare dinner for the family. So he didn't have all day to get them home.

He was halfway there when his wheelbarrow—because this was in Europe, where children used wheelbarrows to bring vegetables home from markets—hit a rock. The wheel—an essential component of a wheelbarrow—cracked. The wheelbarrow would no longer roll. My father needed to get the vegetables home, though, so he needed his wheelbarrow to roll. He spent twenty minutes trying to fix the shattered wheel. He even tried fashioning a replacement "wheel" out of a sturdy vegetable. Nothing worked.

While he was sitting by the side of the road thinking about how much trouble he was going to be in because he was going to show up at home, sooner or later, probably later, without his wheelbarrow loaded with vegetables, it dawned on him that he was trying to solve the wrong problem. He didn't need to get his wheelbarrow to roll. He needed to get the vegetables to his mother. The wheelbarrow was just a convenience. Or, it had been when it had been intact. Broken, it was a hindrance, and spending time trying to fix it was only making his situation worse.

The wheelbarrow, my father realized, could wait. Literally. It could wait there on the side of the road. He could leave it, and it would remain there unmolested, because nobody would take a broken wheelbarrow. So he picked up the sack of vegetables—because of course they were in a sack; one didn't just pile loose vegetables into a wheelbarrow—which he had placed carefully on the ground during his attempts at wheelbarrow repair, slung the sack over his shoulder, and resumed his walk home. It was slower going, but much faster than not going at all. After delivering the vegetables to his mother, he returned to the wheelbarrow with a replacement wheel and the tools to mount it. Then he brought the wheelbarrow—with the tools in it—home. He made it back in time for dinner, too.

While I was asleep, I guess, some part of my unconscious mind realized that I'd been trying to fix a broken wheelbarrow when what I really needed to do was deliver vegetables. And once that had dawned on me, I felt confident that the solution to my actual problem would eventually turnip.

(EARLY DECEMBER...)

I have no formal or informal, or even casual, education or training in any aspect of advertising, or marketing, or otherwise spreading a message to a large group of people, much less trying to convince them of something. I'm not even all that good at or comfortable with self-promotion, to be candid. But I do know letters. I know a great deal about letters, and I have for a long time. At the time in question, as I sat in my office with the dossier from Little, Green open on my desk, I'd already forgotten more about letters than most people ever know about the letters they encounter and employ every single day. The bookshelves around me were filled with hundreds of volumes—of all sizes, though pretty much just the one shape, rectangular—many of them about letters, how they can be used, and how they have been used.

It occurred to me that I probably wanted to have some of those books at hand before I got to work in earnest, so I got up to fetch a few of my favorites. In addition to the modern comprehensive reference guide *Peters on Letters,* I pulled *Littera, Litterae* and *Why, Iota* for the classical perspective and *The Whole Byblos (King Hiram Version)* for the information I'd need on ancient Phoenicia. If you were to ask the average English speaker what ancient Phoenicia has to do with the current-day English alphabet, chances are better than just good they'd say, "Nothing at all." The correct answer, to the contrary, is "Everything." And since I'm a professor, I'll explain why, and at length:

Once upon a time, there was no alphabet. The alphabet—that is, the alphabet as a concept, a set of written letters or symbols, in a fixed order, used to represent the basic sounds of a language—was invented in Egypt around the year 2000 B.C. The alphabet wasn't the first written system of communication, though; Mesopotamia, China, and even Egypt itself at that time had non-alphabetic systems. The alphabet, though, represented a major advance in the efficiency of writing.

In modern times, there are some two dozen major alphabets in use in the world. The Big Three are the Roman, Arabic, and Cyrillic alphabets, each of which serves multiple languages across multiple countries. The Roman alphabet is the most popular with the peoples of Earth, used in connection with about 100 different languages in 120 countries by nearly 2 billion people. Somewhat incredibly, all of the major alphabets of the modern day have a common source in that first alphabet of Egypt, circa 2000 B.C. The Roman alphabet is considered by experts to be second cousin to the Cyrillic, third cousin to the Arabic, and a grandchild of the Greek alphabet.

An alphabet is a writing system employing letters, as every schoolchild knows, even if the schoolchild doesn't appreciate that a letter—the sound of a letter, actually—is the smallest amount of a language possible to isolate, a quantum known by linguists as a phoneme. A phoneme is not the same as a syllable; a phoneme is almost always smaller. Letters by definition symbolize phonemes, and an alphabet, to be effective, has to adequately represent a language by containing enough letters with the right sounds. The essential sounds of that language as spoken, that is. But that's typically not a very large number of letters, both because a given human language doesn't employ many phonemes—only 20 to 40, on average—and because you don't even need 40 letters for 40 phonemes, since letters can and often will do double duty.

Vowels are especially versatile in this regard. Alphabets are amazing things, is the point.

Returning to the Phoenician alphabet, which would eventually become the great-grandmother of the English alphabet, as it were: 19 of our letters can be traced back directly—in their shapes, their position in the roster, and in large part their sounds—to Phoenician counterparts. One expert describes the Phoenicians as a "dynamic Iron Age people." Their homeland was not a unified nation but a grouping of independent port cities linked by a common language, religion, and self-interest. The Phoenicians were Semites, akin to the ancient Jews. Phoenician speech likely sounded much like ancient Hebrew. Israel, the Jewish kingdom of very olden times, was Phoenicia's southern neighbor and trading partner.

Sometime before 1000 B.C., the Phoenicians began writing their language using a 22-letter alphabet. This alphabet was not invented by the Phoenicians but inherited, so to speak, from what's called "prior Semitic tradition." This inherited alphabet, of course, is the one that came into existence in Egypt a millennium earlier. Unfortunately, that thousand years has not provided much in the way of archaeological fodder for scholarly analysis. But the Phoenicians, on the other hand, gave us plenty. One thing we've been able to determine with certainty is that the Phoenician letters, true to the alphabetic principle, symbolized atomic units of speech. And, as it happens, all of the Phoenician letters were consonants. This is not surprising, though. The absence of vowels was a feature inherited from that traditional Semitic alphabet. Biblical Hebrew has no vowels either.

There are two additional fascinating facets of the Phoenician alphabet, one of which has survived, the other of which has not. The Phoenician alphabet had an order. That's the feature that has survived; it's why English speakers all learn our "ABCs" instead of some of us knowing the "PBJs.". The Phoenician alphabet had another mnemonic aid, though: Each letter's name had something—and something significant, literally—to do with the letter itself. Every letter's shape was a depiction of a common item, and the word for that item began with the letter itself. For example: The Phoenician letter that represented the sound "b" (in English) was called "bayt," which was the Phoenician word for house, and the letter looked like a house.

With me so far? Good, because we're really just getting started.

From Phoenicia, the letters of the alphabet traveled to ancient Greece. By boat, most likely. This was around 800 B.C. Now—or, rather, then—the Greeks spoke a language of a different family from the family to which the language of the Egyptians and Phoenicians belonged. The Greek language was in the Indo-European family. (Latin belonged to this family as well, which will be more than just a little important.) The Greeks, like the Israelites, were trading partners of the Phoenicians and, it seems, borrowed several things from them. One of these was the Phoenician alphabet. Of course it was, or I wouldn't have brought them up.

In complete spite of the fact that Phoenician and Greek were very different, the Greeks nevertheless appropriated the 22 Phoenician letters, made a handful of changes (mostly reassigning some letters to different jobs and jettisoning some others), and started writing. This was possible in large part to the flexibility of those letters, and letters generally, as mentioned already. The one really big change that the Greeks made was to invent and insert five vowel letters: the equivalents of A, E, I, O, and U. Years later, the Greeks would fashion two more vowels, but that was after transmission of their alphabet to the Italians, about which more in a moment. First, one final very interesting thing about the Greek alphabet:

The early Greek alphabet followed the Phoenician one in almost all aspects, including the names of the letters. In time, the Greeks tweaked the names of their letters, to make them more, well, Greek. Thus *aleph* became *alpha, beyt* became *beta, gimel* became *gamma, dalet* became *delta,* and so on. But whereas the Phoenician letters' names were also nouns—the words for things whose names began with the corresponding letter—in Greek that wasn't the case. The names of the Greek letters didn't mean anything else. They simply denoted the letters themselves.

Moving on. Just as the Phoenician alphabet could not be confined to Phoenicia, likewise the Greek alphabet could not be confined to Greece. Indeed, it was at pretty much the same time that the Greeks were learning from the Phoenicians that the Italians were learning from the Greeks. Specifically, the Italians of a region called Etruria, whose citizens were called Etruscans, were trading with the Greeks. Archaeologists tell us that Greeks arrived in Italy in about 775 B.C., and Italian enthusiasm for things Greek was especially high among the Etruscans. So circa 700 B.C., when the Etruscans began to write their language, they chose to do so in the letters of the Greek alphabet, which had 26 letters at the time, omega not having been invented yet. The Etruscans, in turn, as the Greeks had done before them, nixed five letters from their borrowed alphabet, since they were not needed to convey sounds in the Etruscan spoken language, and added one, bringing the Etruscan alphabet of around 400 B.C. to 22 letters, the same number as the Phoenician alphabet, which is a coincidence and nothing more.

The Etruscan alphabet then spread across Italy, as these things do, eventually finding its way to Rome, to which all roads lead. The Romans began to write their language—Latin—with the Etruscan alphabet. And, again, because of different needs of the different tongues, changes were called for. Three Etruscan letters were given the boot, others were given new jobs, and a trio of Greek letters were returned to the roster. At the same time, about a third of the letters of the Roman alphabet were reshaped. All of this happened before 250 B.C., when the Roman alphabet contained 20 of our current 25 letters. Still to come were J, V, W, Y, and Z.

The Roman alphabet reached maturity in the heyday of the Roman Empire itself. By 100 A.D., Y and Z had been officially added to the Roman alphabet; by that time, they had been used informally in Roman writing (mostly to aid in communicating Greek words; Y and Z were the Greek *upsilon* and *zeta,* respectively) for some 200 years. Being the newcomers, they were placed at the end of the list. When the Roman letters numbered 22, their sounds were similar to what they are today, and their appearances were identical. That is, the capital letters. The ancient Roman alphabet had no lowercase letters.

We're almost to the present day, I promise. Just one more major development to mark—the birth of English.

Between about 450 and 500 A.D., certain Germanic peoples— Angles, Saxons, and Jutes—invaded Roman Britain and captured most of the territory south of the hilariously named "Firth of Forth." These invaders spoke a Germanic language, naturally, distantly related to modern Dutch, German, and Danish. The moment they set foot on British soil, though, their tongue became known—for all historical intents and purposes—as "Old English." Old English may be considered the "German grandfather" of modern English.

Unlike the Germanic Franks who invaded Roman Gaul (modern-day France) in the sixth century A.D. but who became assimilated by and took the language of the defeated inhabitants (a Latin dialect that would become French), the Anglo-Saxons (I could not tell you why the Jutes don't get equal billing, or *any* billing for that matter) imposed their language onto their new home. This was made much easier in large part because the Roman British did not stick around Roman Britain to see what would happen. They evacuated and left the land to the Anglo-Saxons, thenceforth known as the English. The English had brought with them not just their own language but their own alphabet as well. This alphabet comprised some two dozen letters, which we call runes. Some experts have theorized that the runes—each of them quite angular, since the Anglo-Saxons were carvers more than writers—were born from an adaptation of... you'll hardly believe it: the Etruscan alphabet.

Whereas the spoken language of the English replaced that of the displaced Roman British in Roman Britain, the runic alphabet didn't quite replace the Roman alphabet. Rather, the English appear to have adopted the Roman alphabet, adding to it some of their runes, for the time-honored reason: because their spoken language required it. So the Roman alphabet of the early English grew some. But the Anglo-Saxons weren't the only ones who knew how to show up uninvited. There they were, minding their own business, when in 1066 Roman Britain—now known as England—was invaded by the Normans. The Normans were the people, originally Viking raiders and pirates from Denmark and Norway, who in the tenth and eleventh centuries had given their name to Normandy, a region in France. Their subsequent conquest of England changed that nation forever. Among other things, England received a French-speaking Norman ruling class. Somewhat surprisingly, the conquest did not mean the end of Old English. Old English mixed with the newly arrived Norman French to become what we now call Middle English. The Roman alphabet of Old English mostly survived as well, but not without some casualties. The runes of the Anglo-Saxons didn't make it. One in particular, wyn, was discarded in favor of a Norman letter: W, whose place in the Roman alphabet was secure by the year 1600, bringing the tally of letters to 23.

Norman French also introduced into English one or two sounds unknown to the Anglo-Saxons. One of these would eventually necessitate the advent of J, a typographical offshoot of I. Another would lead to the birth of V, a variation of U. And although no less a personage than Samuel Johnson lobbied vehemently against inclusion of J and V into the alphabet of his day, his formidable influence eventually waned and the last two letters were formally admitted in the mid–19th century, finally bringing the population of the Modern Roman alphabet to the full 25.

If you stayed with me through this entire lesson in the history of letters, I commend you. I fully appreciate that this sort of thing doesn't fascinate most people. Perhaps you, too, can become a crypto-linguist!

(LATE DECEMBER...)

"Guilmard was *not* replaced by an alien," I announced.

First to react was Bradford, who sighed.

"That is good news!" Smith said. "Who is Guilmard?"

"I thought you weren't coming back," Iris said.

"I had a change of heart," I said.

"The next time you quit," Bradford promised, "I'm taking your credentials."

"There won't be a next time," I assured him.

"We'll see," Bradford said. "Now what's this about Guilmard?"

"Yes," Smith put in. "Tell us how you know Guilmard is not an alien, and also who is Guilmard?"

Ah, right, I thought. Smith and Iris didn't know about the Englishman of letters. I brought them up to speed.

"And you thought someone was impersonating him on the telephone this morning?" Smith asked when I had finished.

"But now you don't think so?" Iris asked in turn.

"Actually, I still think it wasn't him," I explained. "I just don't think it was anyone from another planet."

"Then who?" Bradford asked.

"The same person who took the spacecraft debris out of here the other night," I answered, "before getting on a plane to England in time to speak with me today."

Bradford, Smith, and Iris Lucas looked at me, waiting for me to continue. I was a little disappointed.

"...to speak with me in a British accent," I elaborated.

"Sanderson," Iris said, finally.

"Sanderson," I said. "He has a British accent, right?" I knew Sanderson as well as Smith knew Guilmard.

"Yes," Iris confirmed. "But he's in New Mexico..."

"Is he? You told me that Sanderson didn't want me on this project, and I didn't give that a second thought, because I figured anyone would be justified in not trusting me after the whole hoax thing. But Sanderson didn't actually have a problem with me. He just wanted you to second-guess your decision to recruit me, so that your suspicion would be on me when the shard disappeared. Long enough for him to leave the country, anyway. Sanderson had an alibi—he's supposed to be in the desert out West—but he never went. He waited until Bradford brought me to Area 50. Then he grabbed the evidence of the crash and took it home."

"But why?" Smith asked. "What value does the shard have for Sanderson?"

"And how does Guilmard factor in?" Iris asked. "How would Sanderson know that you would want to speak with the man who discredited you, and what purpose did it serve Sanderson to speak to you in Guilmard's place? And how would Sanderson even have taken Guilmard's place?"

I didn't have the answer to any of these questions, but Bradford did me a favor by interjecting.

"I have ideas about all of that," he said. "Let me look into it. Meanwhile, I'd like you three to focus your attention on the evidence of the crash again."

"How?" I asked. The evidence was in England with Sanderson.

"Show him," Bradford said, as he walked out of the conference room.

"We made copies!" Smith said proudly, in the Science Room. Iris had brought in a resin replica of the fragment.

"It doesn't do *me* any good," the archaeometallurgist said, "but I can work from all the data I collected as soon as we got the original under every kind of scope there is."

"Neat," I said. "And I don't have to worry about breaking this."

"Actually," Iris said, "you do. These replicas are molded from man-made materials. Human-made, I mean. Nothing fancy, either. We just wanted to preserve the shape faithfully. Drop one the wrong way, though, and it'll shatter. But the real one," she added, "you could never have broken that."

"Well, something did," I reminded her.

"Sure," she conceded. "A high-velocity collision with the surface of the planet. But I mean that *you* couldn't do damage to that hull."

"Ah," I said. "Well, I'll be careful with this, then."

For the next couple of hours, I carefully turned over the piece in my hands, under my eye, investigating the markings specifically, until I'd come to no conclusion about them and realized that, somehow, they didn't have my full attention. There I was, holding a replica of an alien spacecraft hull fragment—a copy of an actual fragment I'd previously made a point of not holding in my own two hands—and yet I couldn't help thinking about the most mundane things. Human things.

Trust. Dishonesty. Theft. Security. Betrayal. Crime. International intrigue.

I was absentmindedly fingering the letters cut into the hull fragment. D E F G H I

Aitch.

It was just supposed to be a lark.

No one was going to be hurt. Words can cause harm, but a letter?

There was no way anyone could have been harmed. It was a harmless hoax. We all would have had a good laugh afterward.

It all would have been OK. *OK, U C?*

U C I M BZ?

I M A BZ B!

But I wasn't. I had a distraction, but I'd had a career. A promising career. And I'd lost it all, for a lark.

I M N S, I thought. *I C that now.*

"Everything all right?" Iris was standing right in front of me, waving her hand before my eye.

"Sorry," I said. "Deep in thought."

"Anything worth sharing?" she asked. "Anything I can help you with? As I said, there's not much for me to do until we get the original specimen back."

"Then why stick around?" I asked her. "I mean... why not get some fresh air?"

"I can take a hint, Professor," she said.

"Oh, no, no!" I protested. "I'm not trying to get rid of you. Not at all. I'm just... wondering why you're cooping yourself up down here unnecessarily."

Iris softened, much to my relief. "I guess... I guess I just don't know where else I'd go."

"Are you joking?" I asked her. "Smith," I called, figuring that the old German scientist must be somewhere within earshot. "We're going upstairs. To the museum."

"Wunderbar!" he called back. "I will meet you at the elevator!"

Maybe it would be for the best that Smith was coming with us, I thought. Being alone with Iris among the intoxicatingly extensive taxidermy and effusive praise of the twenty-sixth President of the United States might have prompted me to say, or even do, something less-than-professional. The sobering presence of the diminutive, disheveled, heavily accented man of science would remove any possibility of romance from the situation. We would be three uninvolved temporary colleagues clearing our heads together in the American Museum of Natural History.

"Professor Carp," Smith said once we were all in the elevator and the door was closed and there was no escape for the next minute, "Doctor Lucas is an attractive single woman. Perhaps you would enjoy taking her out on a date?"

Iris made a sound I can't describe and which I almost didn't hear over the clank of my own jaw hitting the floor of the elevator car.

"Smith!" I exclaimed. "That's... that's not... we're not... I'm not even..."

Iris rescued me. "Let's see how this outing goes," she said. "As our chaperone, you have a very important responsibility, of course, Smith: You have to keep an eye on Professor Carp's hands."

As she stepped out of the elevator first, she said over her shoulder, "Jeremiah, you keep your eye on the exhibits."

This, I thought, *I don't need.*

A week earlier, I'd been engaged to be married to a woman I'd loved. Still loved. Leah hadn't done anything wrong, after all. Certainly, she hadn't done wrong by me. I showed her that I was not husband material, and she ended our relationship. Even if I wanted to be angry with her, I couldn't justify it. I screwed up and paid the price.

If the Universe was now giving me a shot with Iris Lucas, I didn't want it. I didn't deserve it, and it felt wrong in every way. And, really, right then I just wanted to look at dinosaur bones and remember a much simpler time. My youth, I mean, not the Triassic, Jurassic, or Cretaceous periods, although those were also simpler times, in their own ways. If you were a dinosaur, you were either a carnivore or an herbivore, generally speaking. If you were a carnivore, you needed to be faster than the slowest herbivore, or you'd starve. If you were an herbivore, you needed to be faster than the fastest carnivore, or you'd be eaten.

But that's not quite true. If you were an herbivore, you needed to be faster than

at least one other herbivore. Of course, every day there would naturally be a new slowest herbivore, so being merely second-slowest would have been a very short-sighted strategy...

"Carp!" Iris was calling me from several yards ahead. "You coming?"

"Yes, *Bummelant,*" Smith called in turn. "Catch up!"

Thus distracted from my musings about meat-eaters and plant-eaters, it would take me a little while longer still to remember the lesson of the wheelbarrow and the vegetables.

(EARLY DECEMBER...)

A fence.

If I was to give this new letter a proper pedigree, a thorough history, one that would appear legitimate even if it wouldn't stand up to any real scrutiny, then I had to start at the beginning, and that meant Phoenicia, where the letters of the alphabet looked like things that were called by names that began with those respective letters of the alphabet, I trust you remember. To my eye, this letter had looked like a fence. Not a particularly effective fence, not a fence that a sheep or goat or other medium-sized animal couldn't just slip under, or hop over, but a fence all the same. And since my mission wasn't to critique the stockading skills of the ancient Phoenicians, I'd decided that the figure made a good enough fence, and a fence was a good enough invented inspiration for the figure.

Wait. The Phoenician fence might actually have been a better fence indeed, I realized. The symbol I was looking at would be the *evolved* letter, not the original. The original might have had more components, more lines, more... whatever the horizontal parts of a fence are. Rails? Maybe thousands of years ago it had had three rails: a top, a middle, and a bottom. Maybe it had been in fact a *lot* of fence.

My reference materials revealed that the Phoenician word for a fence was *ket*—pronounced with a guttural k. That presented a problem, being that I wasn't looking to persuade people to adopt the letter K—but of course I wasn't going to find a Phoenician word that started with a letter that I was only pretending had existed in Phoenicia. While I was thinking about how to reconcile this, or fudge it, I found myself ruminating on the ironic fact that I was working on a history for a fake new vowel for the Modern Roman alphabet when the Modern Roman alphabet, at least as used to communicate modern English, could actually use a new vowel.

Linguists—phoneticists and phonologists specifically—know that besides the "long" and "short" versions of the five full-fledged vowels sounds in English (and other languages also, admittedly) there is another, a so-called mid-central vowel sound, usually unstressed. It's the *a* in *about,* the *e* in *taken,* the *i* in *pencil,* the *o* in *eloquent,* the *u* in *supply.* Linguists call it *schwa*—a name derived from a Hebrew vowel—and have adopted as its symbol a lowercase e, rotated 180 degrees. Schwa, despite its apparent utility, has not been invited into our alphabet. On the other hand, we have at least one and a half redundant letters in the list. Consider that hard C, K, and Q all do the same job. Other than the fact that people are generally resistant to change, there's no good reason not to reassign all of Q's duties to K, and then maybe turn Q into schwa. Or C, since S can take over the other half, the soft half, of its work. But we're never going to do that.

What must it have been like to live at a time and in a place when and where the alphabet was changing, naturally or otherwise? One night, you might go to bed familiar with 22 letters, only to wake up the following morning to learn that now there's a *thorn* in your alphabet. It's been runed! (Believe it or not, I hadn't thought of that joke before that day in my office. I'd have to remember it for the spring semester. My students would know what *thorn* referred to: the *Y* in *Ye Olde Shoppe.* That *ye* was pronounced *thee,* just as *you* was once pronounced *thou.*)

The thorn in my side just then was the disconnect between the name of the Phoenician fence and the vowel sound I was trying to relate it to. Any vowel sound, for that matter. Maybe it was almost that simple, though: The K of *ket* wasn't quite our K—the K of, say, *kite* or *king*. It was a sound that we don't have in English. We have part of that sound... the hard part, the part called the unvoiced velar stop, the part made by shoving air along the rear roof of your mouth. So the other part, the growl in the back of the throat, could be what *ket* had represented. That was sort of a vowel sound. Not quite as vowel-y as schwa, perhaps, but not very consonantal either. Was I thinking about this too much? Probably I was.

To the Greeks who received it, *ket* might have been... *keta*. Or, more likely, just *eta*. And it no longer meant "fence." It no longer meant anything. As far as the Greeks were concerned, it was just a letter. A vowel, to the extent that they cared about such distinctions.

Now I was getting somewhere, and it was exciting. *But what will we call it?* Even though I was still only in Ancient Greece, my brain was looking ahead to the future... the past future, anyway—when the letter would have been known to the people of Roman Britain. *We'll get there soon enough,* I told my brain. *You can't rush faking several centuries worth of alphabetic evolution.*

When *eta* came to Etruria, the Etruscans adopted it, but not before simplifying it—they lopped off the top and bottom rails, leaving just the middle bar, which was sufficient to distinguish the letter from others. The Romans in turn adopted the Etruscan letter, as they did with the rest. They left its appearance alone but changed its name, to... well, here I could have some fun. After all, this was only a pseudo-serious history. So the Romans called the letter HA, and it sounded like a laugh.

That laugh had then echoed from Rome proper to Roman Britain, where it wasn't quieted even when the Normans arrived. Or it might have arrived after the Normans did. Either way, the Anglo-Saxons who still made up the majority of the population would have Anglicized the name of the letter...

Oh.

Oh, that's brilliant, I thought. The then-English people of the time spoke a Germanic language. It wouldn't be impossible that they'd have given a new letter a name that sounded a little German, in the modern sense. I thought I knew just the word, too: *echt.* It's pronounced with that same back-of-the-throat growl as *ket,* and it means "genuine."

Authentic.

Real.

What could be more perfect for the name of a letter that was anything but? (Later, I would stop myself from suggesting that the name of the letter could only be pronounced correctly by keeping one's tongue in one's cheek.)

And the punning possibilities were, to my delight, numerous and profound. If I'd been excited before, I was suddenly *echt-*cited for sure, and I imagined that my would-be patrons would be too.

"Echt now!" they could implore their clients. *"Direct. Correct. Echt,"* they could tout the letter. *"You can't spell—or sell—effectively without echt,"* they could claim.

Heh, I thought. *That's echt-cellent.*

I was still scratching down the last of my notes when I picked up my phone. It would take me a few days, maybe a week, to write up my "findings," but I thought I could give Allan and Alan something to work with even as I fleshed out my sketch of the letter's history and decided when, where, and why it had gone missing in history.

Even as the phone rang on their end, however, I second-guessed myself.

Maybe connecting the letter to Germany just then wasn't the most... sympathetic thing to do. For the letter, I mean. Historical accuracy, as it were—and my strong desire to be clever—might have to give way to the political climate of the time. 1949, I mean.

So what if maybe the Normans had... Normanized *echt,* Frenchified it, making it... *etché?* Or *atché?*

But then the English might have had the final say, re-Anglicizing the letter, just to be difficult...

"We're going to call it *aitch*," I declared when someone finally answered the phone at Little, Green.

"Sounds great!" said that person, and I was reasonably sure it was either Allan or Alan. "Does this mean you're going to work with us, Professor Carp?"

"What's that?" I asked.

"Well," said Allan or Alan, "when we last spoke, you weren't quite sure you were on board. Is this your way of telling us that you're coming along for the ride?"

"Maybe," I said. "I want to. But I can't shake the concern that this ride, as you say, won't end up going right off the rails."

"What might put your mind at ease, Professor?"

"Well, frankly," I said, "keeping my name out of it. If I could help you anonymously, I'd be more than happy to. I'd really have no reservations whatsoever if I could be an unidentified co-conspirator."

"But then we'd lose the benefit of your credentials," Allan or Alan lamented.

"Not necessarily," I countered. "You could still use all of my credentials without using my name. After all, my name doesn't mean anything to Joe Consumer. Just describing my expertise is probably more than enough to impress the layperson. And maybe not identifying your source will even help build the mystery."

"You might have a point," the other man allowed. "And if we want to put your expertise behind our discovery, then I suppose we don't have much of a choice."

"I'm afraid not," I said.

"Then we agree to your terms, Professor... X."

"Or 'Professor Aitch'!"

"Sure. I'll share the good news with my partner right away."

"And I'll get to work fleshing out the details for you. Anonymously."

"Sounds good, Professor. Thanks for calling." And with that, Allan or Alan hung up.

Aitch.

Aitch? Well, that was an odd name for a letter. But why not? So it's different. Different can be good, too. We would just be ushering in a brand new aitch, I thought. "American producers, there's a new vowel available! Curious? Of course you are! So scratch... that... aitch!"

Okay, maybe that wasn't quite the way to go. *Allan and Alan will take it from here,* I reminded myself. I still had plenty of work to do on my end.

(LATE DECEMBER...)

"Smith," I said, "you told me that you've been trying to extrapolate the shape of the entire craft from the one piece you have. But you can't really do that, can you?"

We were standing at the Indricotherium exhibit: a two-dimensional wire outline of a massive herbivore that lived in the forests of central Asia between 34 and 23 million years ago, give or take a million years, and has the distinction of being the largest land mammal ever discovered. In the head of the wire frame was a fossil of the skull of a specimen, but the entire rest of the outline was empty. Iris had expressed an interest in looking at the gems, but Smith and I outvoted her so we could see the really old, really big animal skeletons.

"When paleontologists work with a single dinosaur bone," I went on, "they're also working with what they know about how animals in general and other dinosaurs in particular work, anatomically. You don't have any other reference, though. Right?"

"This is true."

"So you might be just spinning your wheels, Smith," I observed. "In fact..." I must have trailed off into silent thought, because Iris prompted me to continue after a moment.

"In fact?" she said.

"In fact," I said, "what you've been studying might not be part of a spaceship at all."

"It came from space," Iris insisted.

"I'm not saying it isn't extraterrestrial," I assured her. "I'm saying it's not part of a vessel. It's not the medium," I explained.

"It is the message. You've been operating under the assumption that the markings were meant to let humans know that the ones sending their ships to Earth have been to Earth before. But what if the markings are the whole thing?"

"A warning?" Iris asked.

"A reminder, maybe," I said.

"Or a suggestion," Smith offered.

"Whatever it is," I said, "maybe we're missing the forest for the trees. Or, actually, the other way around. While we're trying to see the big picture... well, there is no big picture. There's a small letter, and that's what we should be focused on. And I'm not saying that," I added, "just because that's the only way I'll be useful."

"You've already been very helpful," Iris said.

"Because I haven't broken anything?"

"I told you..."

I cut her off. "You told me that I'd never be able to break the fragment. I could break the replica if I tried hard enough, but I'd never do damage to the real thing..."

"That's right," Iris said.

"And that's the proof!" I said. "Why would just part of a whole spaceship survive crashing to Earth but not the rest? If the craft exploded when it hit the planet, there would be hundreds or thousands of pieces. But we found *one*."

"If the craft exploded in the atmosphere..." Smith started to say, but I cut him off, too.

"Then the fragments would have fallen over a wide area. And the higher up the explosion, the wider the range. But no other fragments have been found. I presume that someone's been looking in an ever-increasing radius around where the one piece was discovered?"

"Yes," Smith confirmed.

"Well, someone should tell them to stop," I said. "Because there's no more to find. We've found it all. The one fragment.

And the one fragment tells the whole story. Or reminder. Or suggestion. Or warning," I said.

Then I thought of something else.

"I have to talk to Bradford," I told Smith and Iris. "Will you two join us in fifteen minutes?"

"Something doesn't make sense to me," I confessed to Bradford in his small office in Area 50.

"Do tell."

"Sanderson says he's going out to the desert, and you take him at his word. But he never leaves Manhattan, because instead of going to the crash site for more debris, he slips in here, sticks the only fragment of debris ever found into his overnight bag, and takes off for England."

"It would seem so," Bradford remarked.

"It seems too easy," I commented.

"Does it?"

"Yes. As if..."

Bradford raised an eyebrow.

"...you let him," I said, and Bradford let his eyebrow drop again. "You *did* let him. Why? Come on, Bradford, stop telling me only half of the story."

"You think I've been letting you in on half, Carp? That's generous. I brought Sanderson in specifically because I expected him to steal our fragment," Bradford said. "I needed to see where he'd take it."

"So you've been keeping tabs on him the whole time? You knew he didn't go to New Mexico? And you know where the fragment is?"

"I have," Bradford said, "I did. And I do. Right now, the fragment is in the home of Great Britain's foremost alphabetician, I presume being pored over by that very man even as we speak."

Great Britain's foremost alphabetician...?

"Guilmard?"

"Guilmard."

"What does he have to do with... that end of things?"

"Sanderson and Guilmard have been working together for years," Bradford said. "They've been colleagues at Lanbridge for nearly two decades. When Sanderson first got his hands on alien spaceship debris showing what appeared, improbably, to be Earth letters, he took it to the expert on the same campus."

"You mean now," I said. But Bradford had said that Sanderson—an astrobiologist—and Guilmard had been working together for years. "You don't mean now. There's more debris. Earlier debris. Another 'craft' crashed before the one that crashed in New Mexico. In England?"

"In the United Kingdom," Bradford said. "But the wreckage disappeared soon after it was discovered."

"Disappeared? And British Intelligence didn't have the wherewithal to track it down?"

"Not once the world went to war again," Bradford said. "There were more pressing matters to be dealt with, and plenty of people believed that if we didn't focus attention on terrestrial matters, whether we had been alone in the Universe was going to become a moot point."

Fair enough, I thought. "But now..."

"Now we're working with our Crown counterparts—"

"Crownterparts," I offered. Bradford pointedly ignored me.

"—to recover the old debris—"

"—using the new debris as bait for the bandits. Brilliant, as our esteemed Crownterparts might say." Before Bradford could rebuke me, I continued: "But then why, if Sanderson and Guilmard are in cahoots, couldn't Guilmard just get on the phone yesterday and try to shut me down himself?"

"I have a theory," Bradford said, "but I don't want to hurt your feelings."

"It just wasn't worth his time?" I guessed. "He had just been handed fresh, hot evidence of alien intelligence making use of one of our terrestrial spelling systems, and he wasn't going to put off examining it to take my call. That makes sense," I conceded.

"And the two of them probably figured that I wouldn't know one British accented man on the phone from another, so Sanderson could just pretend to be Guilmard and see what I wanted."

"If it wasn't worth Guilmard's time," Bradford asked, "why would it be worth Sanderson's? No, my theory was that Guilmard just thinks you're a putz. Is that the word I want, Carp?"

"Yes," I said. "That's the word. Listen," I said, getting serious again, "I've asked Smith and Iris to join us shortly, because I want to float a theory. But I don't want to step on your toes. I also don't want to embarrass myself by suggesting something you already know to be true."

"Let's hear it."

"There are no ships."

"No ships?"

"No spacecraft. No vessels. No crashed ones, anyway. Whoever is visiting Earth... isn't, exactly. What they're doing, rather, is more like planting a seed. Or an idea. So what we're finding aren't parts of a whole. They're just the items we're meant to find. And, more to the point, study."

"Well, we are studying them," Bradford remarked. "You think we're somehow playing into someone's hands?"

"Assuming they have hands. But, yes, they want us to do exactly what we're doing: pore over the fragments that are falling to Earth. That they're sprinkling on our planet. They want us to examine them, to try to make sense of them."

"Why?"

"Because there is nothing else to discover. There is no puzzle. The entirety of the important communication is staring us in the face. Or, more to the point, we're staring it in the face. And the more of us who do—the more people we put on the task, the more people who are exposed to Glyph Two-Six from outer space..."

I waited for Bradford to finish the sentence and reveal that I was, once again, only catching up to him. But he didn't say anything, so I completed the thought I'd begun.

"...the more we're exposing ourselves to them."

"Exposing ourselves?"

"Bradford," I said. "They're trying to get inside our heads and change our minds. Literally. The aliens are messing with our brains."

"Our scientists' brains?" Bradford asked.

"No," I told him. "Everyone's brains. Everyone who looks at their alien symbol. Every person who sees the aitch is a target."

"But that's just a handful of scientists, Carp," Bradford insisted.

"But it wouldn't have been," I reminded him, "if Project Aitch hadn't been nipped in the bud and died on the vine."

(EARLY DECEMBER...)

Allan and Alan had already been waiting for me where we'd agreed to meet up—Diner 49er—when I'd arrived. They were sitting on the same side of a booth, which must have looked strange to anyone who saw them before I sat down across the table.

"Gentlemen," I said, and I doubt that my enthusiasm wasn't obvious. "I have something for you." With an entirely unnecessary flourish, I placed a large manila envelope on the table.

"Excellent!" said Little, allowing his partner to take possession of the envelope. Green didn't open it, but tucked it into a briefcase.

"We'll read this back at the office," he assured me. "We wouldn't want to get any food on it."

"But we have every confidence that it's just what we need," Little said. "And we have exciting news for you, Professor."

"Yes," Green confirmed. "Several of our clients have already expressed not just a willingness to brand products with the new letter, but an eagerness."

"Really?" I asked. "Already?"

"We brought a couple of things to show you," Little said. Green took something from his briefcase and placed it on the table before me. It was a thick, red, rectangular plastic frame surrounding a flat gray screen. In each of the two lower corners of the frame was a large white knob.

"It's a toy," Little told me. "Invented in France, as it happens, and really quite ingenious. Turn the knobs."

I reached out for the knobs with both hands.

"One at a time, at first," Green suggested.

I turned the left knob, and a black—or very dark, anyway—mostly horizontal line appeared, then grew, on the screen. I turned the right knob, and a vertical line started and continued from where the horizontal line had stopped growing. I then turned both knobs at once and created on the screen a truly awful diagonal "line."

"Interesting," I said. Little reached over the table for the device while Green told me more about it.

"The inside surface of the screen is coated with aluminum powder," Green informed me. "A stylus controlled by the knobs scrapes off the powder, leaving the screen darker than where the aluminum remains. The line is really just exposing the darkness inside the device."

"Okay," I said. "And this is for kids?"

"Oh, yes," Green said. I could see out of the corner of my eye that Little was busy with the prototype. "But here's the best part: The American manufacturer is going to call it the *Aitch-O-Sketch!*"

"No kidding?" These guys really did get results quickly.

"They're expecting to sell half a million units next year," Little said. I turned my head to look at him, but he was looking down at the gadget, which he had replaced in the center of the table. On the screen was a perfect depiction of... was that *me*? It *was* me. It looked just like me. Before I could ask how in the world Little had managed to draw so accurately something so complicated with such an imprecise device, and in so little time, Green snatched it up again, shook it vigorously with both hands, and secreted it away again.

"Here's something else you'll get a kick out of, Professor," Little said, and I saw that he had produced from somewhere a sphere. He offered it to me, and I took it. Like the previous item, this one was constructed of plastic as well. It was all black, except for a large white circle on the surface, and in the center of that circle, in black again, was an aitch. Holding it in my hands I tried to think of something to which it was comparable in size. It was smaller than a cantaloupe, but larger than a baseball. A softball, maybe? Or a little larger than that.

"Ask it a question," Green suggested.

"What?"

"Ask Magic Aitch Ball a question," Little said, not making things any clearer. "It's a fortune teller."

"It is, is it?"

"Here," Green said, holding out his hands for the sphere. I gave it to him.

"Will this toy be a success?" he asked aloud. Then he shook the sphere.

Does every new product require shaking? I wondered, then I noticed Green turning the ball over in his hands to reveal a large circular window on the ball, exactly opposite the aitch. Green held the ball out for me to see that there was a message in the window. *Signs point to yes,* it read.

"It's a novelty, of course," Little explained, probably unnecessarily. "But fun."

"Yeah?" I asked. I wasn't sold on it.

"Sure! Give it another try, Professor."

I shook the Magic Aitch Ball and thought, Are the two men sitting across from me insane? Then I looked to the window for the answer. *"Reply hazy try again…?"* I asked the men.

"Ask your question out loud!" Green exhorted me.

"Okay," I said. "Ah… Who will be the next President of the United States?"

"Yes," the Magic Aitch Ball answered me, in its way. *What's on second,* I thought.

"Neat," I said, putting in on the table for Little to reclaim. "Anything else?" I asked. "Anything for adults?" I hoped I wasn't coming across as disappointed, even though I was, a little.

"Not yet," Little said.

"But it's early still," Green added.

"Fair enough," I remarked. "Maybe you could convince people to call the fourth month of the year *Aitch-pril,*" I joked.

"Maybe," Green agreed.

"It's on our list of things to look into," Little said. I was alarmed to see that he was serious.

Making my way back home after meeting with the men from Madison Avenue, I realized that I was being a bit unfair to them, and maybe to myself as well, wondering where all the other aitch-branded products were. It had been only a week or so since I'd told Allan and Alan what the letter would—or *should,* anyway; *could,* at the very least—be called. For them to have gotten two different toy companies on board in that time, with prototypes even, was no small feat, I had to acknowledge. And I had every reason to believe that really was just the beginning of the success of Project Aitch.

It was obvious to me that I was just excited about the prospect of being involved in something as big, as pervasive and persuasive, as altering the face of advertising, even if only for a brief time. Because, after all, we weren't *really* adding a letter to the alphabet.

What if, though?

What if we did decide, as a... not a *nation*—because English is written and read outside of America, of course—and not as a *species*—because a substantial part of humanity does not use the Roman alphabet—but a *population,* let's say... what if we decided to start using a new letter? How would that even get accomplished in this day and age? Would it be put to the people to agree upon? To choose? Would multiple candidates for expansion be nominated and vetted and voted on? Would a decision need to be unanimous, or would a simple majority suffice? Would dissenters refuse to recognize the new letter? Could use be enforced?

I found myself chuckling, as I walked, at the notion of an alphabet police handing out citations for misspellings.

"Is there a problem, officer?"

"Would you mind reciting the alphabet backwards?"

"Z-Y-X-W-V-U-T-S-R-Q-P-O-N-M-L-K-J-I-G-F-E-D-C-B-A."

"Aren't you forgetting something?"

"I don't believe in any 'new letters,' officer."

"Then I'm afraid I'm going to have to ask you to come downtown…"

No, I concluded, *best to let it happen naturally, over time. You can't force something like that. Even if it's for the good of a population. Or a nation. Or even humanity as a whole. As if a single letter could have such influence—*

"Watch where you're going, buddy!"

I was jostled back to the real world by a fellow pedestrian—whom I must have nearly walked into while woolgathering. *Day-b-c-dreaming. Lost in reverie-f-g.*

I have a real problem, I thought, with a chuckle.

But if being constantly on the pun was the worst of my worries, I knew, then I was doing pretty well.

At 9 a.m. on Friday, I'd gotten a call from the secretary to the president of my college. Dr. Miller—my boss, when it came down to it—wanted to speak with me. In his office on campus. Could I be there at ten? Yes, of course, I said, and I tried not to gulp audibly.

"Jeremiah," Dr. Miller said, not at all unpleasantly, "please come in. Take a seat. Do you know Arthur?" He was referring to the other man already in the room, suited-and-tied, sitting in a chair pulled up to the president's substantial desk, the kind and color you'd expect a college president to have in his office. The desk, I mean. The man was not insubstantial, but more than anything he was... humorless. "Arthur Grossman is general counsel to the school."

Ah. A lawyer. My employer's lawyer. This did not bode especially well.

"General counsel," I repeated. "This must be pretty serious," I remarked, trying to lighten the mood of the room, which was currently somber.

"It is," Grossman said. "Professor Carp, the college has received a subpoena requiring you to appear before a congressional committee."

"A congressional...? Not—"

"Not that one," Dr. Miller said, "no."

"That one might have been better," Grossman remarked. "You've been called to give testimony to a subcommittee on fraud in commerce. It seems that someone at the Federal Trade Commission believes you might have insight into consumer deception."

I'd been sweating already, but at this comment, I redoubled my perspiratory efforts.

"I—"

"Jeremiah," Dr. Miller said, rescuing me, some, from floundering, "your recent... extraprofessional activities have been brought to our attention."

In the few years I'd been at Dreyfus, I'd spoken with Dr. Miller a handful of times, only a couple at any significant, memorable length. I had no doubt that he knew who I was and what I taught, but I didn't have any reason to think that he was at all fond of me. Yet it seemed that he was loath to give me bad news. Maybe that had nothing to do with me, though. Maybe he didn't like giving anyone bad news.

Grossman, however, had no compunction about getting right to the point.

"Your work for certain members of the advertising community was noted in the papers served. We obtained a copy of the materials you prepared—at their behest, we understand, for their use. The propriety of the circumstance is questionable, to put it mildly."

"Am... am I being fired?" I asked, genuinely unsure whether or not that was where the conversation, the meeting in my college president's office with the school's general counsel, was heading.

"Not yet," Grossman said.

"No, Jeremiah," Dr. Miller clarified quickly. "But your preparation of materials commissioned by a third party will need to be considered by an administrative review board, given that the materials were to be used in a..." Here Dr. Miller faltered, unsure of the proper phrase. Grossman had it at the ready, though.

"A scheme of deception."

"You understand, I'm sure," Dr. Miller concluded.

"Can we back up a second?" I asked. "Because I'm not sure I do understand. You called me in this morning to tell me that I'm going to have to appear before some members of Congress—the Congress of the United States, in Washington, D.C., I presume—because the FTC learned about an advertising campaign—which, yes, I helped out with by providing some mock-academic material. But in addition to having to testify—about what was explained to me would be a mere, non-academic marketing effort—I might also be subjected to disciplinary action by the college? For a joke?"

"Academic dishonesty is no joke, Professor Carp," Grossman said.

"Academic dishonesty?" I asked. "No one in academia would have believed my material to be genuine! The whole idea was to work up something that laypersons would never actually read and experts would know right away was a goof."

"Be that as it may, Professor," Grossman informed me, "several experts have read your work, and none of them found it amusing."

"Wait," I said. "How did anyone read my work? I only delivered it to Little and Green—I presume you know who they are—earlier this week."

"I don't know the details," Grossman confessed, "but it's plain that the scheme was brought to the attention of the Federal Trade Commission, and that agency in turn notified the appropriate person or persons in Congress."

"It's not a *scheme,*" I protested. "It was a... gag." I found myself quickly running out of ways to characterize the hoax that didn't make it sound despicable.

"You're the expert at words, Professor," Grossman said. "I only know the law. Unfortunately, your words might have gotten you on the wrong side of the law."

"Am I being accused of a crime?" I asked. Because so far no one had said anything about my being accused of a crime.

"No, Jeremiah," Dr. Miller answered, but the lawyer jumped in.

"Again—with all due respect, Doctor Miller—not yet. There has been no suggestion of criminal charges yet," Grossman said, "but that could change. For that reason, you have the right to refuse to answer the questions of the committee. And although I am not *your* lawyer, it does serve the best interests of the college for me to recommend that you exercise that right. You would still have to appear in person before the committee, but once there you could invoke your Constitutional protection against self-incrimination."

My head was starting to spin. "Do I really need to do that?" I asked. "Is the committee looking for me to... confess to a crime? Is what I did actually a crime? What if the committee just wants information? Maybe it's Little and Green they want to prosecute." I was just speculating, of course.

"The committee isn't prosecuting anyone," Grossman explained, "but anything said in the hearing can be used against whoever says it, should prosecution be recommended. We simply don't know what might happen, or who might decide to take what action, down the line. That's why the college would prefer that you, as an employee of the college who presumably wishes to remain in the employ of the college, not answer any questions."

"Oh," I said. "So that's what this is about. You're asking me to keep quiet about... everything. In return for keeping my job."

"There's no guarantee of continued employment," Grossman footnoted.

"But not making things worse, not calling more unnecessary attention to the school, might persuade the review board to clear you of wrongdoing if they're on the fence," Dr. Miller put in, and I couldn't help but wince inwardly at the inopportune mention of a fence. "As Arthur says, Jeremiah, I can't promise anything, but this is an unfortunate circumstance that will need to be addressed. We'd just hate to see it get any worse for you, and for the school as well, of course."

After a moment of reflection, I said, "I understand." And I did. The president of the college and the school's lawyer were being up front with me. I'd done something arguably wrong, and there might be repercussions. I could potentially contain those repercussions, though. My desire to help a pair of advertising men had prompted me to do the arguably foolish thing in the first place; any desire I might have to help the congressional subcommittee investigating those ad men could add fuel and get me fired. I had to stop helping other people and help myself a little.

"When do I need to be in Washington?" I asked. "When am I expected to appear and give testimony... or not?"

"Monday morning," Grossman said. "I suggest you head down no later than tomorrow afternoon. Give yourself some time to settle into a hotel. This is bound to be a nerve-racking experience, even if you refuse to answer questions," Grossman said. "Best to give yourself plenty of time to get there, at least."

And with that final bit of advice, the lawyer stood and took his leave of us. He did not wish me well or even wish me luck.

"Doctor Miller," I said, "I never meant to drag the college into anything untoward."

"Just between you and me," the other man said, "I think this whole thing is absurd. I haven't had the pleasure of reading what you wrote, but from what I do know, it sure sounds like someone's making a mountain out of a molehill. Unfortunately," he added, "sometimes people do that. And then sometimes good people, people who didn't mean any harm, get buried under that mountain."

This was... unfortunate.

Not good.

Bad.

I had to talk to Leah, of course.

But first I wanted to talk to Allan and Alan. One of them, at least. So I called the number they'd given me, where I'd reached them before. A switchboard operator informed me that the number was no longer in service. I realized I had no other way of contacting the men. I found no listing for their firm in the phone book, and the operator couldn't provide me with an address, on Madison Avenue or otherwise. So unless they reached out to me, I would have to wait until Washington to speak to Messrs. Little and Green again.

(LATE DECEMBER...)

"That I was commissioned to fabricate a history and pedigree for a new, invented letter that supposedly wasn't new at all, which then turned out to be a real... thing," I explained, summoning all my available articulateness and breath, "is not a coincidence. The men who hired me to help sell the public on what I dubbed the 'aitch' didn't *anticipate* discovery of Glyph Two-Six. They knew about Glyph Two-Six. They *knew* it had been sent to Earth because *they came from the same place.* Out there. I can't believe I didn't realize it any sooner, but I was working directly for aliens! They'd even pretty much put it on their business cards: Allan Little and Alan Green," I reminded my teammates. "The men from Little, Green..."

"The Little, Green men!" Iris exclaimed.

"I wanted to say it," I grumbled. "But yes. Exactly. Them. And their plan," I continued, "their *idea,* anyway, was to introduce Glyph Two-Six to children. That the two items they showed me as the first to be branded with the aitch were *toys* was entirely intentional. At the time, I thought they just weren't having success in other markets. Adult markets. It didn't occur to me— well, a lot of things didn't occur to me until just recently."

"And the shards?" Iris asked. "You said it's not a coincidence that your aitch and Glyph Two-Six were the same. But they were going to be getting different kinds of attention at the same time."

"Just so. And that attention was going to come from two very different kinds of Earthlings: impressionable children, on one hand, and serious, studious grownups, on the other."

"But why?"

I didn't really *need* the prompts from Iris, but I appreciated them all the same.

"To guarantee greater exposure, I presume. Because maybe one prong of the two-pronged approach wouldn't work. Just as it *didn't,* as it happened. But that's not coincidence either," I added.

"Meaning?" Bradford asked.

"Meaning that it was a serious, studious grownup Earthling who put the kibosh on Little and Green's campaign. A pair of them, really: Sanderson and Guilmard."

"Sanderson and Guilmard are thieves," Bradford protested.

"Thieves, yes," I conceded. "But they're not the bad guys. In fact," I mentioned, "there might not even be bad guys, strictly speaking. There might just be men, and women—and aliens, in whatever varieties they come—with different agendas. But for what it's worth, I suspect that Sanderson and Guilmard only want what's best for humanity—and since we don't know what the extraterrestrial agenda is, exactly, our human colleagues' priority is to keep the alien influences contained, even if that means stealing them."

"So you think the aliens shot another shard marked with Glyph Two-Six to Earth because Sanderson and Guilmard had locked up the first one?" Bradford asked.

"Yes. But I also think that Little and Green—or whatever alien marketing department they work for—didn't have confidence in the dropping-shards-on-Earth plan, which is why Allan and Alan came here themselves and tried something different and much less passive. Instead of waiting for scientists to find alien items and study them and announce their findings over the course of several years, Little and Green thought they'd stick Glyph Two-Six—as the aitch —literally right under the noses of hundreds of thousands of kids at once, hooking them while they're still young."

"But to what end?" I detected a rare hint of frustration in Bradford's voice. "Even if all of this is true, as far-fetched as it is, we still have no idea what the *purpose* of exposing humans to Glyph Two-Six is."

"That's correct," I said. "We do not know what Glyph Two-Six is supposed to do to, or for, humanity. And, unfortunately, studying the character itself isn't likely to give us the answer. But fortunately," I added, "there's another way to get the answer."

"And that is?"

"We ask someone who knows," I said.

"And who knows the answer?" Iris asked.

"Sanderson and Guilmard?" Bradford asked.

I smiled.

"Smith," I said, and I pointed at Smith, who hadn't said a word the entire time we four had been in the room together. "Oh, didn't you realize?" I asked Bradford and Iris. "Smith isn't from around here, of course, but he also isn't from Germany. Smith," I said, "like Little and Green, is from... out there."

No one gasped.

"*I* am an alien?" Smith asked.

"Smith? I don't think so," Bradford asserted. "I vetted Smith myself."

I was undeterred. "You don't think an alien with the means to insinuate himself into human society could create convincing credentials, Bradford?"

"What makes you think Smith is an alien?" Iris asked me.

"It was something he said," I told the group. "Do you remember forgetting the English for 'jigsaw puzzle,' Smith? You knew the German word: *Zusammensetzspiel*. But that's not the word a German would use. A German would just say 'puzzle.' My grandmother was German, and my mother speaks some German. My mother has never said *Zusammensetzspiel*."

Smith just looked at me for a moment, his lips pursed. He didn't seem angry. He didn't seem disappointed. He just seemed... calm. Finally, he said, "I am not from another planet, Professor Carp."

I looked at Smith for another long moment. Then I said, *"Damn it. That would have solved everything."* I could see Bradford shaking his head. "But just so we don't have to do this again later: Is anyone here an alien? Raise your hand if you are." No one raised a hand. "Fine. All the other stuff I said is true, though. Unfortunately, without any alien input, I think we've reached the end of what we can figure out."

"Then it's time we moved this research party," Bradford declared.

"Move it?" I asked. I looked at the others, and each of them seemed to be accepting Bradford's declaration as obvious. Only I questioned relocation, it appeared. "To outer space?" I asked with some concern.

"To England," Bradford said, and he, Iris, and Smith looked at me like I didn't have a doctorate.

"To confer with Sanderson and Guilmard," I said. "Of course."

"We leave tonight," Bradford informed us. "It's a fifteen-hour flight to London, mostly over water. There will be precious little to see out the windows, so bring a book if you can't sleep in an airplane seat."

"Iris, can I talk to you?"

"Only if you're not going to accuse me of being a Martian," she warned.

"Don't be ridiculous," I countered. "Women are Venusian. But seriously: I'm a little anxious about this fifteen-hour flight."

"You don't like flying, Carp?"

"I don't know," I confessed. "I've never flown before."

"Ah. Then, no, you're probably *not* going to enjoy this one. Unless..."

"Unless?"

"Well, if Smith isn't holding a grudge, I'd bet he can find or make something to knock you out, and thoroughly."

"I know just the thing!" exclaimed Smith himself, who evidently had overheard our conversation. I turned to see him smiling at us. "Where I come from," he said jovially, "we call it 'Barbital.' It's a sleeping aid first synthesized by my people by condensing diethylmalonic ester with urea in the presence of sodium ethoxide—"

"I know what Barbital is, Smith," I muttered.

Iris chuckled as she walked away, leaving me alone with the man I'd just a few minutes earlier suggested was from another world... yet who was still willing to be kind to me, albeit at the price of ribbing. Smith leaned in close toward me, poked me in the side with a finger, and whispered, "I also don't enjoy the long flights. If you know what I mean, Earthling."

"Look, I'm sorry about that, Smith," I said. "It was a shot in the dark."

"Believe it or not, Professor Carp," Smith said, "I am flattered. Being from anywhere 'around here' is not such a thing to be proud of these days."

I laughed, a little. I knew what Smith meant. "Do you think," I started to ask, but then thought better of it and told Smith to forget it.

"I will not be able to forget it, Professor Carp. You had better finish your question."

I sighed and did as the older, wiser man suggested. "Do you think, Smith, that maybe we'd all be better off if aliens did come to Earth and take over? Humans aren't exactly doing a terrific job of things, left to our own devices. Our own devices are becoming more and more destructive, in fact. Maybe a little supervision wouldn't be the worst thing in the world for the world. Our world."

"Perhaps not," Smith said, "but in my experience a little supervision does not stop there. Over*seeing* has a way of becoming over*powering*. When we learn how to behave and no longer need to have an eye kept on us, do you think humanity's alien minders will graciously accept our invitation to leave?"

"I suppose not," I conceded.

"No," Smith said. "Humans will have to figure out how to get along with one another without help."

"And if we don't?"

"Then the Universe will have to get along without you."

I cocked an eyebrow at Smith.

"Us!" he corrected himself. "I mean without *us.*"

Because I awoke in what appeared to be a rustic cabin and because Harry S Truman himself was there with me, I realized that I had not in fact awoken at all but was, rather, still heavily sedated and somewhere over the Atlantic Ocean with hours to go before we landed in England. Because I did not want to rock the boat, so to speak, I played along. I sat up in the armchair I was sitting in, wiped some drool from my mouth, and said, "Mister President. It is an honor."

The other man said, "I am not your President Truman."

I winked at him—exaggeratedly, because a regular wink from me doesn't look any different from a blink. "I know," I said, then added, "sir."

"No," he said, evincing more exasperation than I was used to seeing in constructs of my preconscious mind. "My name is Vister."

"What?" I asked. "Why?"

"Because that is my name!" he insisted. "And I have brought you here to discuss your involvement—"

"Wait," I said. "You say your name is 'Vister,' but you look almost exactly like President Truman." I could now see that he did look very much like Truman but wasn't quite a *doppelgänger*. Still, the resemblance was uncanny, and I told him as much.

"Meaningless coincidence," Vister said.

"I'll take your word for it," I said. "Now, your name: Slavic?"

"No," Vister said. "Alstromerian."

"I'm not familiar with that language."

"That is not surprising," Vister said. "It has never been spoken on this planet."

"One more question, Vister the Alstromerian who looks like Harry S Truman: Where are we supposed to be?"

"You are supposed to be on an airplane, I understand," Vister said, "but because I abducted you from your home before you could join your friends for the flight, you are now in my secret, remote mountain outpost. I have brought you here to discuss—"

"This is a secret, remote mountain outpost?" I asked. "It's a log cabin. I mean, isn't it? I don't have the best vision, but I know a log cabin when I'm inside one. The large logs that make up the walls are a dead giveaway."

I thought Vister might have been grinding his teeth. "Yes," he said. "We are in a log cabin."

"I'm not judging," I assured him. "Your secret, remote outpost can be anything you want it to be. I just wanted to be certain that you and I are seeing the same things. And the mountain?"

"What?"

"You said this is a secret, remote *mountain* outpost. What mountain are we on?"

"Does that matter?"

"No," I said. "But I'm curious all the same."

"I believe the nearest mountain is called 'Sweet... bread?'"

"Sweetbread? Do you mean *Sugarloaf*? We're in the Catskills?"

"I guess. I don't really know."

"You don't know if we're in the Catskills? You have a remote, secret mountain outpost but you don't know where it is? Are you the one it's a secret from?"

"I'm just using this place to interrogate you," Vister confessed. "I don't own it!"

"You're interrogating me?" I asked. "Has that begun yet?"

"We can begin as soon as you stop asking questions about my appearance, my name, and my methods!"

"I'm sorry," I said. "I was just trying to make conversation. It's not every day, or night, that I get to talk to a figment of my imagination."

"I am not a figment of your imagination!" Vister insisted. "Where do you think you are?!"

"Your remote, secret mountain outpost, of course," I said with another wink.

"Stop doing that with your eye! This is not a dream! You are not asleep. You are not flying to Europe. You are awake, and you are going to tell me what you know about The Gramideon and how you know what you know."

"The Gramideon?"

Vister sighed with what sounded like contempt. "You referred to it as 'aitch.'"

"Oh," I said. "You mean Glyph Two-Six."

"It is The Gramideon," Vister corrected me.

"Whatever. You know everything I know," I suggested, admittedly a bit grumpily. "Can't we talk about something else? That letter-that-isn't-a-letter is pretty much all I've been thinking about recently. It would be nice to have a distraction. No?"

"No," Vister said, "I did not go to the trouble of transporting you from your domicile to this place to talk about anything else. I want to know why, of all the people on Earth, you apparently have a unique insight into the importance of The Gramideon."

"But I don't!" I said, and now I was getting frustrated. If my brain was trying to work something out while it had the opportunity, I couldn't fault it for that, but it was getting under my skin in the process. "Allan and Alan gave me the symbol. I don't know who gave it to them."

"I know where they obtained The Gramideon. And I know why they brought it here. What I don't know—the only thing I don't know—is why they brought it to *you*."

"They said they needed—"

"They said they needed someone to help them make The Gramideon appealing to your people, I imagine. Yes. But why you?"

I didn't care for the insinuation. "Why not me? And what's the difference, at this point? It didn't work. The whole initiative was a bust."

"I know," Vister said. "I busted it, to use your vernacular."

"*You* did."

"I did. I brought my fellow Alstromerians' plot to the attention of your authorities before it could even approach fruition."

"Your fellow Alstromerians?"

"We are from the same place, the three of us," Vister said, "yes. But we are not of the same opinion about the worthiness of your race to receive The Gramideon again."

Well. My brain was working overtime to confuse me, it seemed.

"Hold on a second," I said. "Please." I wasn't sure which part of what Vister had just said to ask for clarification of first, so I just picked a part randomly: "My... race?"

"Humanity," Vister clarified, "as you refer to yourselves."

"And the worthiness of my... of humanity?"

"To receive The Gramideon," Vister put in.

"*Again*, I think you said. Because we *did* receive it before. From you?"

"Not from me, certainly," Vister assured me. "And not from my people. But from another people we know."

"I know them?"

"No. We, the Alstromerians, know them. I'm referring to the Cosmic Etymistics. They first fashioned The Gramideon and imbued it with the power it has."

"To enclose livestock," I said, nodding.

"It is not a fence!" Vister shouted. "How do you see a fence in the symbol? Are you—"

"Blind? Only half."

"I was not going to say blind."

"Sure," I said. "But you were saying that it's not a fence..."

"The Gramideon," Vister explained, "represents two beings—two enlightened beings, two beings who have evolved beyond the need for competition—standing before one another and clasping appendages in a gesture of solidarity."

"They're shaking hands," I said.

"Sure. They are shaking hands."

"Okay, I can see that. And you say it has a power?"

"It has the power to promote cooperation."

"That's it?"

"What do you mean?"

"I mean, the great power of the symbol—"

"The Gramideon."

"—is to suggest to people who see it that they should work together? That they should get along?"

"Yes," Vister said.

"And humanity is not worthy of such a device?"

"Recent Human events suggest otherwise."

"That's some circular logic," I countered. "Because we don't get along, we're not worthy of getting along? Maybe recent events prove that we need The Gramideon more than we ever did."

"Maybe I misspoke," Vister conceded. "It is not that Humanity does not deserve The Gramideon. It is that Humanity does not deserve to survive. The peoples of Earth are destroying each other—and themselves—at an accelerated rate. Left to your own devices, Humanity will remove itself from the Universe in short order." *I had just said the same thing to Smith!*

"And you're okay with that."

"I am all for it," Vister said. "I think the Universe would be better off. I think the Universe *will* be better off."

"Will be. When?"

"Fifty years."

"Fifty of our years?"

"Yes. At your present rate of self-destruction. But Humanity has a gift for exceeding expectations." Vister's sarcasm surprised me. It did not delight me.

"I think you underestimate us," I told him.

"I think you aren't seeing the whole picture," Vister said, adding, "no offense. I, for one, am happy to let Humanity remove itself from existence. There are some who want to help remove Humanity. And they are on their way."

"Here?"

"Here," Vister confirmed. "Earth. Where Humanity is." Again with the sarcasm.

"Now?"

"Now. I cannot tell you when they will arrive, but I can tell you that if Humanity is still here when they do, they will not be pleased."

"And you, Vister?" I asked. "I don't suppose you'll be here when they arrive."

"Absolutely not," he said. "In fact, I am leaving Earth now."

"Are we done here, then? Did I answer all of your questions?"

"Actually," Vister said, "I think you answered none of them. I am not even sure I got to ask any. No matter."

"Well," I said, ready to be finished with this unreal conversation, "safe travels, 'Vister.' I can show myself out."

"No, you cannot," Vister said.

I awoke in my own bed, in my own apartment, and not in a plane somewhere over the Atlantic Ocean *en route* to England. I realized that I had not been dreaming. Possibly. I really didn't know what to think. So I headed straight for the only place where it felt right for nothing to quite make sense.

(EARLY DECEMBER...)

Of course Leah had cried, but that hadn't prevented her from coherently conveying her reasons for breaking off our engagement.

"You discarded your entire career," she said softly.

"It should never have come to that, though," I protested. Feebly. "I agreed to work for Little and Green on the express condition that my name would be kept out of their... *everything*. My identity was going to be protected. I was going to provide the 'research' for a fictitious 'expert.' I made them promise that my contribution would be anonymous. And as far as I know," I added, "they didn't go back on their word. So this never should have happened."

I waited for what felt like an interminable stretch of time for Leah to say something, but she said nothing. I knew what she wasn't saying though, and she was right. *But it did happen.*

"I'm sorry," I told her.

"We were going to have a family. We were going to build a life together on the foundation of your stable employment. Maybe that's not fair, but that's the way it is, Jeremiah."

A line of argument occurred to me. What didn't occur to me is that arguing with Leah is not what I should have been doing just then.

"What if I'd lost my job because Dreyfus decided not to offer classes in my field any longer? What if that happened five years into our marriage? Or ten years? Would you pack up your things and leave me?"

"Of course not!" Leah replied. "Not if you lost your job through no fault of your own. I wouldn't care if you were out of work, if it were just that. I'd stand by you unemployed as well as if you were president of the college, or even president of the country. But this is different. You're not likely to be hired somewhere else now. No one is going to take on a disgraced academic... and you could have avoided this tragedy entirely!"

"I tried—"

"No. You asked the men who offered you an opportunity to have some fun—your kind of fun, specifically—to protect your good name—and I'm sure you were perfectly polite about it, too—but what you should have done was protect your good name and turn them away. You can't just take chances with your future. Our future. What you did was completely... irresponsible," Leah said. "And I can't marry an irresponsible man, even if I love him.

"I'm not going to spend the rest of my life wondering... worrying that my husband is going to jeopardize everything we have just for some amusement."

I didn't remind Leah that she'd recently offered to join me in playing practical jokes on my family. I saw the difference between that and this.

"Not everyone likes the same jokes," Leah said, almost as if she knew what I was thinking. "Not everyone has the same sense of humor. The men in charge at the college, it would seem, aren't laughing about having an accused fraud on the faculty, tarnishing the school's reputation. I don't suppose the advertising men have offered you a job?"

I couldn't tell Leah that I couldn't reach Little and Green. "No," I said. "But I haven't actually lost my job at the college," I reminded Leah.

"You will," she predicted. "I love you, Jeremiah. I always will. And I hope you eventually land on your feet."

And then Leah gave me back my ring.

"I don't understand, Jeremiah," my mother said. I'd called her as soon as I'd gotten home from Leah's apartment. "You're no longer engaged?"

"I'm afraid not, Ma. I screwed up," I said. "I screwed up badly."

"I don't even understand what you did, Jeremiah. Leah won't marry you because you want another letter in the alphabet? What do you need another letter for, Jeremiah? What you need is a wife."

I took a deep breath. My mother was not a simple woman. She could understand anything she cared to. But when she heard something that she didn't like, or that she even suspected she wouldn't like, she simply refused to comprehend it.

"I don't want another letter in the alphabet, Ma," I said, "but the letter isn't important right now. What's important is that I tried to help some men and it got me into some trouble at work, and I also have to go down to Washington and appear before a Congressional subcommittee in a couple of days, and I could lose my job, so Leah ended our engagement. Because she can't trust me to be responsible. And... and I really screwed up, Ma," I said. "And I don't know what to do now."

My mother didn't say anything for a moment, but when she did respond she said, "Yes, Jeremiah. You screwed up, badly. And as much as I want to take your side, I have to tell you that I agree with Leah. You did give her reason to wonder if she could ever trust you again. And it's a very smart woman—a very strong woman, stronger than most—who can put aside the fact that she loves you—and believe me, she still loves you—for the fact that she worries that she'll never know when she should trust you and when she shouldn't. You should *never* give her a reason not to trust you. Because nothing should be more important to you than her."

I thought she might be finished, but my mother had more to say.

"You're a smart man, Jeremiah. You're a very smart man. The smartest thing you can do now is give Leah some time to cool down, to maybe forgive you some on her own, without you begging her to do it. Leave her be. And anyway, it sounds like you have a more immediate problem. Because Leah isn't likely to get engaged to anyone else in the next couple of days, or even the next week or the next month. So you'll have your chance to apologize and persuade her, prove to her that you deserve a second chance, but in two days you're expected in Washington. Some very serious men are going to be asking you some very serious questions about a very serious thing you probably should never have gotten mixed up in. So you're going to need a lawyer.

"Your cousin Sammy is a lawyer, Jeremiah," my mother told me. "I'll get you his number."

"Law Office of Sam Fisher."

"Sammy? It's Jeremiah Carp. I'm your second cousin. My mother and your father are first cousins. My maternal grandfather and your paternal grandfather were brothers."

Yes: My mother had been a Fisher before she'd landed a Carp.

"Jeremiah," Sammy said. "I know who you are. You were there when I became *bar mitzvah*."

"That's true. I wasn't sure you'd remember me, though."

"Well, I remember you more because you're the son my father wishes he had."

"What? That's ridiculous. Why?"

"Because you're a college professor."

"You're a *lawyer*. Also, I only have one working eye."

"That's in your favor too," Sammy said. "Somehow."

"Your father wishes he had a cycloptic academic for a son instead of an attorney with proper binocular vision?"

"Hiram Fisher might be the only Jewish father in New York City who doesn't believe that practicing law is any kind of job for a nice, Jewish boy. And he thinks that being half-blind has only made you try twice as hard to succeed. So, naturally, I've been hearing about you my whole life."

"Well, then, you'll be happy to know that when Hiram hears the latest, he'll probably change his opinion about me," I told my cousin. "I need your help, Sammy. I need a lawyer, at any rate. I've been subpoenaed to testify down in Washington."

"For real?"

The question struck my ear as somewhat casual, but I responded in kind. "For real."

"About what?"

I told him.

"When's the hearing?"

"In two days. In the morning."

"So we'd need to head down tomorrow afternoon?"

"I guess we would. Can you?"

"I suppose I can. Business happens to be very slow just now. It's the dead of winter," Sammy said, "but people just aren't slipping and falling like they used to."

"Wait," I said. "You're *that* kind of lawyer?"

"I'm every kind of lawyer."

"Sammy, I'm not sure—"

"Jeremiah, I presume that your employer knows about the subpoena?"

"It was served on the school's general counsel."

"And he didn't offer to accompany you?"

"He probably would have fired me already if he had the authority. The president of the college likes me, though."

"Did the president offer to have the school hire a lawyer for you?"

"He did not."

"Do you know how much lawyers charge?"

"I don't," I confessed, "but I suspect it's more than I'd be happy to pay."

"You have no idea. Which is probably why your mother suggested that you call me. Jeremiah, we're family, even if we haven't seen each other in twenty years. Look, I'll be straight with you: I've never been to D.C., and I wouldn't mind being able to tell prospective clients that I've represented someone at a Congressional hearing, even if I probably won't have to do very much in reality. So I'm willing to do not very much work for free."

"Ah. So then you are exactly the kind of lawyer I'm looking for," I told my cousin.

"You'll just pay my expenses," Sammy told me. "Train fare, room, meals, and maybe a souvenir."

"It's a deal," I said. "You're hired, Sammy. Even though I'm sure he would enjoy hearing that I'd opened my mouth and shot myself in the foot," I mentioned, "the school's lawyer told me not to answer any questions. I presume you'll tell me the same."

"The school's lawyer wants what's best for the school," my cousin remarked, "but, yes, keeping quiet is what I recommend as well."

"I don't really need you, then, do I?" I asked him.

"Not really," Sammy said. "But it's too late; you've already retained me. And you don't want to disappoint your mother, I'm sure."

"If I disappoint her any more today, she might disown me."

"That," Sammy said, "I understand." And I believed him, even if I couldn't believe that his father would have preferred that he'd become a teacher. *Rabbis* were teachers. And everyone knew that being a rabbi was no profession for a nice, Jewish boy.

(LATE DECEMBER...)

There was no one present at Area 50 when I arrived—which lent more credence to the notion that I'd been left behind by my colleagues, who must have had no idea at all why I didn't board that plane overseas with them—so there was no point in my being at Area 50 either. I was just coming to this obvious conclusion, and taking one last look around before departing again, when I heard the elevator chime, signaling that I was about to have company in the secret government laboratory-cum-mission center under the Museum of Natural History. Who else would be arriving but my teammates, I thought. So they must have decided to delay the flight when I hadn't shown up. I was momentarily embarrassed by the realization that they considered me indispensable.

I was embarrassed when the elevator doors opened to reveal not Bradford, Smith, and Iris Lucas, but two men, each holding a strap on either end of a large steamer trunk. A pair of Bradford's underagents?

"You!" I said, because I recognized one of the men. I surmised who the other man must have been. "What the hell are you doing here?"

Vincent Guilmard and Silas Sanderson stepped out of the elevator car and put the trunk down.

"We're looking for you, actually, Professor Carp," Dr. Guilmard said, a little out of breath. The trunk must have been plenty heavy, and Guilmard was not a young man.

"And the others," Sanderson put in. "Where are the others?"

"The others, Sanderson? You mean the rest of the team you double-crossed, ripped off, and abandoned? They're in..." I snapped my fingers, pretending that I needed to recall the whereabouts of the Area 50 crew. "...England!" I said, making the revelation mockingly dramatic. "London, in fact. *Looking for you*. And," I added, pointing to the trunk now at our feet, "what I presume is in there."

"They're looking for me?" Sanderson asked.

"For both of you," I said, mentioning, "They know you've been working together to collect and hide the shards. The shards *are* in the trunk, right?"

"Yes," Sanderson acknowledged.

"Why?" I asked.

"Why?"

"Yes," I said. "Why are you carrying around with you, in broad daylight, the alien artifacts you've been taking pains for decades to keep out of sight and out of the hands of anyone who might want to examine them?"

"Because we've recently—very recently—come to the conclusion that we may have been taking the wrong pains for decades," Sanderson said, sheepishly. "And we need help fixing our mistake."

"Do you. Well," I said, "you showed up at the wrong place at just the wrong time, I'm afraid. Try back in a couple of days, when the people you ran out on have returned from their wild English goose chase."

"But you're here now," Guilmard remarked.

I looked at him, then at Sanderson, then at Guilmard again. They were waiting for me to say something.

"But I hate you," I said, finally. "Okay, *hate* might be too strong a word," I followed up. *"I really do not like you*. Either of you. Each of you went out of your way to make me look very bad, and you did a damned good job of it," I reminded them, though I didn't think they'd forgotten.

To their credit, Guilmard and Sanderson looked contrite.

"We are very sorry about all of that," Guilmard said. "But it was absolutely necessary."

"You were being too obliging!" Sanderson explained, as if that explained anything.

"Sure," I said. "I understand. So how can I help you gentlemen?"

My sardonic tone was not lost on the Brits.

"Carp," Guilmard said, "please believe that it was misery for me to publicly call your abilities and intentions into question. I have nothing but respect for your work. I was even thoroughly impressed by the very efforts that I had to expose and deride. But I did have to expose them, because the figure you dubbed *aitch* is dangerous. Potentially dangerous, anyway. Or so we believed," he conceded.

"Glyph Two-Six is an unknown," Sanderson offered, trying to support his compatriot, "at best."

"Maybe not completely unknown," I countered. "I had a theory," I told them, "that Glyph Two-Six—which I think we all agree did not originate on Earth—was given to humans, intended to alter human nature. And then my theory was confirmed, just last night, by an alien who claimed to be familiar with the ones who gave us the gift. At first I thought I was imagining him," I confessed, "but then it turned out that I wasn't. I had in fact been abducted and brought to a log cabin for questioning by an alien who looks like Harry S Truman."

Guilmard and Sanderson exchanged glances.

"You... you spoke with an alien last night, Professor?"

"Perhaps we will just come back in a couple of days..."

"You know they're here," I asserted. "Three of them, at least. I've met three of them, anyway. The first two are the ones who got me involved in the first place. The shards are from outer space. So are the two men who want those shards to serve their intended purpose, and so is the one man who wants the opposite."

"But we still don't know what the shards' purpose is, what Glyph Two-Six is for."

"I do," I said. "Vister told me."

"He told you?"

"He told me. He told me that it has the power to... guide us—humanity—to a more peaceful future."

"And—Vister, you say?—is not keen on that idea?"

"He is not. He'd prefer to see us all gone."

"Why?"

"He's kind of a jerk," I said. "Every intelligent race has jerks, I guess. Look, I can't explain aliens. But he also mentioned that we have limited time to get our act together. Very limited time."

"But then why..." Guilmard trailed off.

"Why what?"

"Why didn't it work?"

"Why didn't it... because you stopped it, Guilmard! You helped, anyway. Vister said that he was the one who alerted the authorities to the scheme. I'll give you the benefit of the doubt and assume that you were not working with him."

"I was not," Guilmard assured me. "But I mean why didn't it work the first time? Presuming that what we suspect is true, that an alien symbol was introduced to the literate people of Earth before now, and that symbol was, to some greater or lesser extent, integrated into written communication, and it was your *aitch*."

"And if it was Glyph Two-Six," Sanderson picked up the thread, "and if Glyph Two-Six has the power to make those who employ it more... cooperative with each other, then why did the peoples of Earth just have the largest armed conflict in the history of the peoples of Earth? Why didn't Glyph Two-Six pacify us? Or at least civilize us more?"

"Are you asking me?" I asked Sanderson and Guilmard. "Because I don't have the answer to that. My *aitch* is not *my aitch*. I'm taking your word and Vister's that The Gramideon, as Vister insisted on calling it, made an appearance on Earth before this century. My own research turned up no evidence to corroborate this theory. And I have to imagine that neither of you have seen Glyph Two-Six in the wild."

Guilmard and Sanderson exchanged another glance.

"Guys," I said, "I think we're past the point of your needing to exchange knowing glances before letting me in on a secret. Just tell me what you know. Exchange knowing glances on your own time, if you don't mind."

"We haven't seen Glyph Two-Six in print," Guilmard informed me, "but I have long heard and read rumors of a single existing item in which it appears. Unfortunately, in forty years I have been unable to find this item. It is reportedly kept safe by a guardian so fiercely protective that the item might as well *not* exist, because the guardian will never permit it to be seen by any other person, for any reason. Again, though," Guilmard added, "this is just hearsay and conjecture."

I laughed.

"Carp?" Sanderson asked.

"I think I know where to find the item we're looking for," I said. "Unfortunately, its guardian might prove to be even more protective than you have heard. And I'm afraid he's already not a big fan of mine."

"Lead the way, Doctor Carp," Guilmard said.

"Wait," Sanderson interjected. "The shards."

"They can stay here, can't they?" I asked. "This is supposed to be a secure facility. Even though you still have access, for some reason, after deserting the team and stealing the very object they were brought together to study. Your key really still works, Sanderson?"

"I got down here without a problem," he said.

"So you did. I really wonder about Bradford sometimes," I commented. "All of the time, really. Let's move the trunk out of the way, at least, so that nobody trips over it, even though nobody else should be arriving before we get back. You just never know with this group."

(EARLY DECEMBER...)

"Jeremiah," my cousin the lawyer had said, "repeat after me: *On the advice of counsel...*"

"On the advice of counsel..."

"*...I invoke...*"

"*...I invoke...*"

"*...my Fifth Amendment privilege...*"

"*...my Fifth Amendment privilege...*"

"*...against self-incrimination...*"

"Wait."

Sammy and I were seated opposite one another in our compartment of the *Marylander*, on a four-hour rail trip that would take us through Pennsylvania, Delaware, and the train's namesake state to Washington, D.C. Because the Baltimore and Ohio Railroad didn't have direct service across the Hudson River into Manhattan, we'd begun our journey that afternoon by boarding a bus at Columbus Circle. Our train was now hurtling my cousin the lawyer and me southbound toward my first visit to our nation's capital and what I'd expected would be one of the most keenly uncomfortable experiences of my adult life. And Sammy was preparing me for it.

"What?"

"Is that really what I'm doing? Avoiding self-incrimination?"

"Well, if you're not, then you don't have a privilege to invoke. So you need to be."

"You're saying I'm actually better off if I could get myself into trouble by opening my mouth?"

"You can look at it that way, yes. Because there's no Constitutional protection against mere self-embarrassment, so if you're only worried about your reputation, then you probably have to give answers. Lucky for you, this subcommittee will be asking questions about consumer fraud—which is a crime. And I'm sure I don't need to tell you that *crime* is at the heart of *incrimination*."

"From the Old French, *crimen,* meaning 'judgment' or 'offense,' based on the Latin *cernere,* 'to judge.'"

"Sure, Jeremiah. Whatever you say. But when you're sitting before a panel of angry elected officials who want to know about your part in a recent attempt to trick the American public into buying things they might or might not need or want, what you want to say is: *On the advice of counsel, I invoke my Fifth Amendment privilege against self-incrimination and respectfully decline to answer your question.*"

"Got it," I said.

"I'll write it down for you. It's perfectly acceptable for you to read the statement."

"Not necessary," I assured my cousin. "I've memorized entire orations by Cicero and poems by Catullus."

"Have you?"

"*Quo usque tandem abutere,*" I quoted, "*Catilina, patientia nostra? Quam diu etiam furor iste tuus nos eludet? Quem ad finem sese effrenata iactabit audacia?*"

"Lovely," Sammy said. "Truly... poetic."

"Actually," I mentioned, "that's the start of a political speech. Cicero is asking Catiline when he'll stop abusing the patience of the Senate, how long his madness will mock them. That sort of thing."

"What did Catiline do to deserve that sort of vitriol?" Sammy asked.

"He bribed Senators to elect him to a consulship. Allegedly," I added for Sammy's benefit. "And other unethical conduct. Like conspiring to murder Cicero and key members of the Senate.

Cicero, fortunately, discovered the plot and had martial law declared, which then gave him absolute power."

"Cicero," Sammy clarified. "And Catiline?" he asked.

"Accounts differ. Supposedly he went into a self-imposed exile, but some reports say that he retreated into the company of the treasonous military force that had been assembled to overthrow the Republic. He was declared a public enemy. Eventually, he died."

"I figured as much," Sammy said, "since he lived three thousand years ago."

"Less," I said. "The start of the Roman Republic is dated at 509 B.C. And Cicero gave his four Catiline orations toward the end, about thirty-five years before the start of the Empire."

"Wait."

"What?"

"The Roman Empire came *after* the Roman Republic?"

"Yes."

"Not the other way around?"

"No. The Roman Kingdom gave way to the Roman Republic, which in turn gave way to the Roman Empire. They were all part of what we loosely refer to as the ancient Roman civilization."

"Huh," Sammy said.

"Huh?" I asked.

"I'm just amazed at what fills your head. So much knowledge in there," he said.

"And zero common sense," I added.

"Can I ask you, Jeremiah," Sammy said: "What did you think was going to happen? What was your best-case scenario? Fortune and fame? Radio appearances? Your statue in the Hall of Hoaxes in the Museum of Linguistics?"

"Sammy," I said, "you'll forgive me, but I'm just not in the mood to talk about it right now. I talked to my bosses about it, and they're not happy. I talked to my fiancée about it, and now she's not my fiancée any longer. And then I talked to my mother, and that might have been the worst of all the talking about it, somehow. And tomorrow, I'm going to specifically not talk about it to members of Congress, so I don't go to jail, or worse."

"There really isn't a possibility of worse," Sammy put in. "Conspiracy to commit fraud—even on the entire country—isn't a capital offense."

"Fine," I conceded. "So I won't be hanged or shot or given the electric chair. I still just don't want to talk about it anymore right now."

"Then say it."

"What?"

"If you don't want to talk about it, tell me the right way, Jeremiah."

Ah.

"Mister Fisher," I said, "on the advice of counsel, I invoke my Fifth Amendment privilege against self-incrimination and respectfully decline to answer your question."

"Perfect," said my cousin the lawyer. "You're ready."

When about half the trip had passed, perhaps to minimize the opportunities for further awkward conversations in close quarters, Sammy had done the valiant thing and closed his eyes for a nap. I wasn't in the mood to follow suit, but I also didn't want to stay there, awake, in a compartment with my sleeping cousin, so I exited the room and went looking for a distraction elsewhere in the train. The *Marylander* was famously well-appointed, offering numerous passenger amenities, none of which I found tempting just then—which was too bad, since I couldn't have said when I would next be on such a singular vehicle.

Indeed, besides the air-conditioned coaches, the parlor cars with private drawing rooms, the full-service dining car, the deluxe lounge cars, and the onboard telephone and radio services, the Marylander had just two months earlier made history by becoming the first moving train to offer onboard *television* reception. In early October, the second game of the

World Series was enjoyed (probably; maybe just watched) by the *Marylander's* passengers, along with a Federal Communications Commissioner, news reporters, and B&O officials. I didn't know if anything was showing that afternoon, though, and in any event, I probably wouldn't have been able to sit still for it. Likewise the radio. And there was no one I wanted to call. So I wound up at a table in the dining car, behind a cup of strong coffee.

At first, I thought that I was—improbably—alone in the car, but then I noticed someone else, at a different table. That is, I assume it was another person and not just the hands I could see holding up a newspaper in more or less exactly the way one does when one does not want one's face to be seen, but when one doesn't care or mind that one's hands are exposed to scrutiny, if not identification. As far as I could tell, calling upon all of my powers of observation, it was a man behind the paper. The hands—and the paper—were still for another minute, until one of the hands disappeared for a moment. To turn a page, my hearing told me. Then the hand appeared again. These were indeed exciting times.

When I finally focused my attention on the paper itself, I saw the headline on the front page:

TOKYO TOJO NO MO'
Japanese War Criminals Executed

I shook my head and rubbed my neck with my hand simultaneously, at once amazed at the flippancy of the *News* or *Post* and sincerely hoping that my cousin the lawyer was right about participation in a conspiracy to put one over on the country not being punishable by death.

To clear my head, I took a gulp of my drink and a look out of the window at the scenery flashing by—Delaware, I guessed, though probably not for long— and when I turned back again the man at the other table was gone. His newspaper was flat on the table, closed. I really didn't want to read it, but something compelled me to retrieve it, take it back to my own table, and at the very least thumb through it. Had I thought I'd discover a message in the tabloid, a secret communication meant for my eye only? It wasn't likely, I knew, but what if that mysterious other man had left something for me to find, and had specifically been mysterious to make sure I would find it?

I looked in the paper. I found no message for me, hidden or otherwise. I did find a crossword puzzle, though, so I solved it. Without a writing implement.

Eventually we pulled into Union Station. Sammy—whom I had to wake with a familial shove—and I collected our valises, disembarked, and took a cab to our lodgings at the decidedly less-than-regal Royal Octavo Hotel. Not that I'd expected luxury. I was paying for our lodging, and I'd decided that good enough was more than good enough for the likes of us.

(LATE DECEMBER...)

"No, no, no," the librarian was saying. He'd already said it at least a hundred times, varying his inflection some of the time, but never varying his straightforward message of denial.

"This is a matter of life and death," I said. "Of every human on Earth. Eventually."

Sanderson and Guilmard were standing behind me as I beseeched my nemesis at the New York Public Library's Rare Book Division. For the moment, they were keeping quiet, trusting me to handle the situation. "You *have* to let us see the book," I all but whined.

"First of all," the librarian said, "as I've already told you, I am not at liberty to confirm the existence of any such volume or text that might or might not be the one you describe."

The volume or text I had described to him had been described to me by Guilmard. As Guilmard had not corrected me, I presumed that nothing had been lost in translation.

"In the second place," the librarian said, "when you were here earlier this week, you left something behind. Perhaps you realized that you are missing something?"

I had realized nothing of the sort and admitted as much.

"When I inspected the *Biblia Latina* after your visit, I found in its pages an eyelash. One of yours, yes. And now you've brought two other men with you? That's entirely too many eyelashes to risk finding in my rare books. I'm afraid I must ask you all to leave at once."

I was still processing what the librarian had just told me when I felt a tap on my shoulder. "May I?" Guilmard whispered in my ear. I stepped aside to let him speak with the intractable librarian, and I silently wished him luck.

"My good sir," Guilmard said, and I knew immediately that he had no hope of prevailing. One cannot fight pedantry with politeness. While Guilmard entreated the librarian, I reflected on the librarian's mistake: not simply advising us that the volume (or text) we sought was not in the Library's collection. If he had lied to us believably, we would have just left, disappointed. But his officious refusal to confirm or deny the existence of the item we sought told us that it existed, there, in the library.

There was another tap on my shoulder. My other shoulder, this time.

"What is it, Sanderson?" I asked.

But it wasn't Sanderson who answered.

"Perhaps I can be of assistance. A word with you," the new man said to the librarian. It wasn't a question. And as I watched the librarian step out of the room to speak with—or, rather, be spoken to by—none other than Agent Bradford of the United States Government, I knew we were going to get to see what we'd come to see.

While we waited, Guilmard, Sanderson, and I spoke with Smith and Iris Lucas, who had arrived at the Library with Bradford. After the necessary introductions, Iris asked me, "What happened to you, Jeremiah?"

"I'm a little hazy on the details," I admitted, "but it would seem that I was abducted by an alien."

"That's very exciting!" said Smith.

"It really was. It was also very strange. But informative," I allowed. "Why aren't you in England?"

"Bradford told us, when we got to the airstrip, that we weren't actually going to England," Iris said.

"That sounds about right," I commented. By this time I'd completely given up on trying to understand Bradford's intrigues. We were all just his pawns, but at least with him in control, we did appear to be always moving forward. "On a related note," I said, "it turns out that Sanderson here didn't actually double-cross you, and Guilmard did not actually intend to malign me publicly. So all of that's behind us now. Except, of course, that when this is all over, I still won't have a job…"

"We will see," Guilmard told me. "I will speak to your college president if you think that would help."

"That probably would help," I said. "Thank you."

"It is the very least I can do," Guilmard said, and I agreed with him.

"Everyone," Smith said, "he's coming back.

The librarian returned to where we were waiting. He came back alone. I had never before and I have never since seen a man look so defeated. And yet the librarian also seemed to be relieved, as if a great burden had been lifted from his shoulders, his conscience, or both.

"If you will be kind enough to follow me to the Clean Room," he told us, "I will make the item you were inquiring about available for your inspection."

Well, that was terrific news.

"Indeed," the librarian added, "if you desire, you may relocate the item from the premises."

"We can borrow the book?" I asked.

"You may," the librarian confirmed. "Indefinitely."

Well, that was incredible news.

"Mister Bradford asked me to inform you—"

"Wait," I interjected. "Did he say his name is 'Mister Bradford'?"

The librarian thought, despite seeming surprised and perturbed by the interruption. "No," he answered, finally. "He introduced himself as 'Agent Bradford,' as I recall."

"Darn," I said. "I'm sorry. Please continue."

"Wait," Guilmard said. "Do you not know the name of your man you're all working with?"

"It's his last name," Sanderson said. "Isn't it?"

"It could be his first name," I suggested. "He could be Agent Bradford..." I looked around for inspiration. "Shelf... man."

"Bradford Shelfman?" asked Iris Lucas. "That seems unlikely."

"I agree. But my point is that if Bradford doesn't like his surname, he'd be more likely to use only his first name. Smith," I asked, "you know things no one expects you to know. What do you know about Bradford's name?"

"I am afraid I know no more than the rest of you," Smith said. "Perhaps we should permit our patient host to finish his report, though, yes?"

No one had any objection, so the librarian continued: "Your friend asked me to tell you that he had other business to attend to, and that he will rejoin you in due course." To our collective credit, the group did not take issue with the characterization of Bradford as our friend.

At first, none of us was willing to touch the book, but finally, I said, "Look, it's just a book. The cover isn't telling us anything."

The cover of the heavy (we imagined, based on its thickness), old (we assumed, based on how old it appeared to be) volume—a deep burgundy leather hide—had no markings on it. It was impressive but uninformative.

"I will open it," Guilmard volunteered, "if I may. I have been looking for this book my entire adult life."

"Please," I attempted to encourage him.

Guilmard extended a cotton-gloved hand—we were all wearing cotton gloves, provided to us by the librarian, who had shimmied away afterward—and then withdrew it.

The rest of us exhaled.

"I can't," Guilmard said. "It's too important. Silas? Would you—"

Iris leaned forward over the table we were all standing around and flipped open the front cover of the book.

"What do you know, guys?" she said. "Nothing bad happened! It's not cursed or booby-trapped. Now, would someone like to read what it says? I would try, but I'm just an archaeometallurgist."

I scowled at her, good-naturedly, then joined Guilmard and Smith who were already scrutinizing the text.

But we *couldn't* read it, as it happened. There was a lot of text, and it was all in extraordinarily small print. We would need an industrial-strength magnifying apparatus.

"To the lab?" Smith proposed.

"Just an archaeometallurgist, huh?" I asked Iris Lucas as the group made its way back to the Museum of Natural History. (Guilmard was given the honor of carrying the tome; he had it clutched to his chest, under his very British greatcoat.) "Is that what you wanted to be when you were a little girl?"

"Of course not," Iris told me. "Like most other little girls, I wanted to be an actress. Or an anthropologist."

"But definitely something that starts with A?"

"Yes. And then... oh, you know what happens. You get to college and think you're on the path that the Universe has chosen for you, only to be diverted by opportunities to explore ancient iron production. You just don't know temptation until you're wrist-deep in centuries-old smelting waste, and you can practically smell the non-ferrous slag in your mind's nose..."

My mind's... nose?

"Are you making fun of me?" I asked.

"No," she said. "Why would I be? Anyway, I ended up with an undergraduate degree in Chemistry for Women, with a certificate in Theoretical Cuppelation, and went on to do my doctoral work in the field of study I'd fallen for, lock, stock, and beryllium."

"Is that... is that an archaeometallurgy joke?"

"I'm afraid so," Iris said.

(EARLY DECEMBER...)

"Good morning, and welcome to today's hearing, entitled 'An Inquiry Into an Attempt to Enlarge the American Alphabet.'"

According to the nameplate in front of him on the dais, the man addressing the rest of us in attendance in the hearing chamber—an impressive but not overlarge room—had been Mr. O'Mahoney, chairman and ranking member of the Consumer Vigilance Subcommittee of the U.S. Senate Committee on Interstate and Foreign Commerce. The other members of the committee were, from my left to my right: Mr. Vandenberg, Mr. Wherry, Mr. Young, and Mr. Taylor. For the most part, the chairman and ranking member did the talking.

"The purpose of this hearing is to examine a recent attempt to introduce a new letter into the alphabet as used in this country, with the goal, as the subcommittee understands it, of providing producers of consumer goods and services an additional means of identifying or branding those goods and services and thereby making them more likely to be purchased by consumers. And specifically, we wish to consider whether the proposed preparation and promulgation of propaganda purporting to prove the propriety of promoting a pretended lost letter was improper." The other members of the panel murmured their assent to this summary.

"Before we continue, I want to note that the subcommittee has no intention of interfering with or impeding any investigation that might be conducted by any federal agency, bureau, commission, or department. We urge everyone's cooperation with any such investigation, and I thank all of our witnesses for appearing today and look forward to their testimony."

I almost couldn't hear anything after "any investigation that might be conducted" because of how loudly my heart was beating in my chest. Sammy, who was seated next to me at the witness table, put a hand on my shoulder. That helped.

"Now, we are on a tight schedule this morning," Mr. O'Mahoney continued, "so we're going to hear from the witnesses out of the intended order, since Doctor Guilmard has not yet arrived, but Doctor Carp is here. I will now swear in Doctor Carp.

"Doctor Carp," Mr. O'Mahoney said, "would you please stand and raise your right hand?"

I looked at Sammy, who nodded. I stood. I raised my right hand.

"Do you solemnly swear or affirm that the testimony that you are about to give is the truth, the whole truth, and nothing but the truth, so help you God?"

I leaned forward and down a bit, to speak more into the microphone at my seat than toward the dais generally, and stated: "On the advice of counsel—"

Sammy abruptly put his hand over the microphone and shook his head at me, whispering, "Not yet."

"I do," I said when Sammy had removed his hand from my microphone. Then I sat again.

"Doctor Carp," Mr. O'Mahoney asked, "was that a preview of what we can expect this morning?"

I looked to Sammy. Sammy spoke into my microphone. "Samuel Fisher, Esquire, New York City, New York, counsel for the witness. With all due respect, sir, yes, it is."

Mr. Mahoney appeared to mull this revelation over for a moment, looking around to his colleagues. Then he said, "The subcommittee understands. What I'm going to do nonetheless is proceed with my questions and give Doctor Carp the opportunity to respond to each individually. But, under the circumstances, I will limit my questioning to those matters most pressing to the panel.

"Doctor Carp," the senator began, "the subcommittee recently had brought to its attention certain academic materials—or, I should say, materials seemingly of the academic variety—with the name of Doctor Jeremiah Carp, Professor of Crypto-linguistics at Dreyfus College, attached to them. The subject of the materials in question is the alleged discovery, by the author, of a certain letter, called 'aitch,' that at one time was a part of the Modern Roman alphabet but which, for reasons hypothesized in the materials, was lost. Are you the author of those materials?"

Although it seemed harmless for me to answer this one preliminary question, my cousin the lawyer had explained that answering any question, even one that seemed harmless, would "open the door" to further questions, and that the door could not be shut, so I should not let the door be opened even a crack.

"On the advice of counsel, I invoke my Fifth Amendment privilege against self-incrimination and respectfully decline to answer your question."

"Doctor Carp, the subcommittee understands that you were approached by two persons who identified themselves to you as advertising men, and who asked you to help them with an initiative to add a letter to the alphabet, in a manner of speaking. Can you confirm that you were so approached?"

"On the advice of counsel, I invoke my Fifth Amendment privilege against self-incrimination and respectfully decline to answer your question."

"The subcommittee has attempted to locate the so-called advertising men I just mentioned, but to no avail. Do you know where or how they, or either of them, might be reached?"

I didn't. I wished I did. And I wanted to tell the subcommittee as much.

"On the advice of counsel, I invoke my Fifth Amendment privilege against self-incrimination and respectfully decline to answer your question."

It went on like this for a full five minutes. It felt like an eternity. Finally, Mr. O'Mahoney thanked me for attending—and he did not sound at all sarcastic, to his credit—even though I really had had no choice but to attend, since disobeying a subpoena is contempt, legally speaking, as my cousin had explained to me. Then the panel turned its attention to the man who had arrived, I realized only then, while I'd been refusing to answer questions and who had taken a seat at the witness table on the other side of Sammy. I could hear him, but I couldn't see him well without craning my neck. I didn't want to eschew decorum by wriggling about in my chair at a Congressional subcommittee hearing, though, so I remained still, and curious, while the other man cast—heaped, really—aspersions on me.

"Doctor Guilmard," Mr. Mahoney said, "please accept the subcommittee's most sincere thanks for being present this morning. Before I pose my questions to Doctor Guilmard, I want the record to reflect that when the subcommittee sought an expert on the alphabet, the staffs of our members reached out to numerous authorities in this country. To a man, every domestic expert recommended that we speak with Professor Vincent Guilmard of Lanbridge University in London. Because Doctor Guilmard will testify regarding events that took place before the American Revolution—well before, in fact—the subcommittee has no reservations about hearing from a non-citizen expert on the matter. Indeed, the subcommittee is honored that Doctor Guilmard agreed to give testimony and that he was willing to be here today in person."

Well, I thought, *if I'd gotten an introduction like that one, I might have admitted to having shot President Lincoln in Ford's Theater.* I knew of Vincent Guilmard. He was, without question, England's premier letter authority. What I didn't understand was why the subcommittee—or anyone—would need information about letters—real letters—from any authority. Certainly, the subcommittee wouldn't be able to learn any more about the plans of Allan Little and Alan Green, or either of them, from Guilmard.

Mr. O'Mahoney administered the witness's oath, then got right to the point:

"Doctor Guilmard, are there any 'lost letters' of the alphabet. The alphabet used to write English, I mean."

"There are, sir. Most students of the alphabet would agree that four letters have been, as you say, lost from the Modern Roman alphabet. But when we say that these letters were lost, we do not mean that they are no longer known. We mean that they are no longer used. But we are fully aware of them."

"Can you tell us about these four letters?"

Guilmard told the panel about *thorn, eth, wyn,* and *yogh*— the supplementary quartet of Anglo-Saxon signs used to represent Old English sounds that were not covered by the traditional Roman letters. Use of the Anglo-Saxon letters had gradually ended after the Norman Conquest of England, due to pressure exerted by Norman-educated clergy and teachers who had sought to infuse written English with a more sophisticated (Guilmard's word, he noted, not necessarily the teachers') Franco-Roman form. The last of the set to disappear was thorn, used minimally into the nineteenth century, but then, with its three noble kinsmen, lost.

"And the letter known as 'aitch,' Professor?"

"There is no letter known as 'aitch,'" Guilmard said. "There is no letter that looks like that symbol, by that name or any other."

"Are you aware of any evidence to support a claim that any letter, by any name, resembling the symbol at issue or not, has anything like the history set forth in the materials authored by a Doctor Jeremiah Carp?"

"I have read the materials you refer to, and I found them to be thoroughly unsupported and unsupportable. The claims made are not merely unsubstantiable but dangerously so."

Dangerously unsubstantiable?

"Not to put too fine a point on it," Guilmard asserted further, "but in my entire career as an alphabetician, I have never read anything so emphatically and indefensibly fallacious."

There was more—there was *much* more, somehow. Fortunately, mercifully, the years have allowed me to forget the rest.

"Mister Chairman," Sammy said into my microphone. "My client wishes to make a statement."

Senator O'Mahoney looked at his watch, then said, "He may proceed."

"Gentlemen," I said, "having now listened to the testimony of Professor Guilmard, with whose warranted reputation as an alphabet authority I was already familiar, I feel compelled to make it unequivocally clear that I was at no time asserting—other than as part of the marketing initiative the panel is aware of—the existence of a truly 'lost' letter. 'Aitch' was at all times a fabrication. Whether this was a good idea or not, the entirety of the idea was to pretend, briefly, that a lost letter had been found. The intention of the pretense, however, was never to convince anyone permanently that the alphabet—our alphabet, the Modern Roman alphabet, for which I have nothing less than the utmost respect—needed, or needs, any enlargement. My contribution to the scheme, from start to finish, came completely from my own brain, though based of course on factual research, and my understanding is that the design of the letter, the new letter, was likewise wholly the product of the imagination of some other person or persons unknown to me."

"Doctor Carp," Mr. Mahoney responded, "you understand that by knowingly making a voluntary statement addressing the subject of inquiry of this hearing you have waived your right to further invoke any privilege against self-incrimination and must now respond meaningfully and truthfully to any and all questions posed to you by the subcommittee or else be held in contempt?"

I looked at Sammy. He made a face that said, *You just made your bed. Now lie in it.*

"I understand, Senator." *So be it.*

The Senators conferred, briefly, and then Mr. Mahoney leaned toward his microphone. "The subcommittee has no further questions for Doctor Carp. You are excused. That concludes this hearing. We are adjourned."

I didn't get to speak to Professor Guilmard afterward. I didn't want to speak to him, really; I would have said things I might have regretted, sooner or later. For better or worse, then, he slipped out of the chamber just as he'd slipped in, and I figured it was just as well that I didn't have a chance to clear the air with him. Or push him down a flight of stairs, which is what it felt like he'd done to me.

(LATE DECEMBER...)

Back at Area 50, we—Guilmard, Sanderson, Smith, Iris Lucas, and I—convened in the main examination area—the good ol' Science Room—and placed the library book on the expansive examination table there. Smith brought over a large magnifying lens mounted atop a free-standing swivel arm and positioned the glass directly over the first page of the volume, enabling us all to see what was on it.

"It's Latin," Sanderson said.

"It's not Latin," I said, but perhaps a bit too curtly, because Guilmard immediately added, "But it was made to look like Latin."

The minuscule—that is to say tiny, not lowercase—text of the first page of the manuscript—an illuminated manuscript, about which more in a moment—began *LOREM IPSUM DOLOR SIT AMET,* which, to be fair, is and is not Latin. Some of the words were, and other words appeared to be parts of, Latin words, but the syntax of the "sentences" was not Latin syntax.

"Very curious," Guilmard remarked. "It could take weeks, even months, to make heads or tails of this." I suspected that Guilmard would have enjoyed that, actually. But something was telling me that it would be a waste of time. A distraction.

Beside the hundreds—more likely *thousands*—of painstakingly neatly handwritten words of strange, possibly insignificant quasi-Latin was a single panel of illumination, a full-color illustration of a simple scene: In the foreground stood two men—both apparently military men, maybe even one ancient Roman centurion and one ancient Greek hoplite, each with a sheathed sword on his belt—facing each other, clasping arms in decidedly non-aggressive greeting. In the background was a mountain range. A bright yellow sun shone on the men from a clear blue sky above.

"The men," I said. "They're forming The Gramideon. Glyph Two-Six."

"So they are!" Smith exclaimed.

"So what, though?" Sanderson asked, and I will readily admit that I was thinking the same.

"Shall we turn the page?" I asked.

When we did, we were surprised—again—by what we found. Because what we found was exactly half of what we'd expected to find. What we found on page three of the volume was, more or less, more of the same, but there was nothing on page two. That is, the reverse of the first leaf of the book was blank. And a quick flip through the remainder of the leaves told us that the entire book was like that: Only the rectos had been used.

"Why?" Iris asked. None of us knew, though.

"It might have made sense," Guilmard said, "if the text had been printed on a press, which marks just one side of a sheet of paper at a time. The printer might have been hesitant to run each sheet through a second time for fear of tearing it. But that clearly isn't the case. Even more curious."

So we turned our collective attention back to the fronts of the book's two hundred or so leaves. On the second right-hand page was another illustration, similar to the first but with a couple of differences: the men shaking hands under a sunny sky were not soldiers, but appeared to be farmers in a field. One of them was considerably darker-skinned than the other.

On the third decorated page, there were two of these scenes, and on successive pages there were either one or two, in varying positions on the pages. The men—and women—included persons of all shapes, sizes, and shades, and the settings for their moments of harmony varied as well, representing diverse geographies and landscapes, although the weather was steadfastly consistent. The illustrator must have had a lot of blue pigment to use up before it dried up, I thought.

"I suggest we take a break," Smith said. "Come at this from a different angle in a little bit, yes?" The others concurred. One by one, Iris, Sanderson, and Guilmard filed out of the room.

"You won't mind if I stay, will you, Smith?"

"Of course not, Professor Carp. You won't mind if I do as well, will you? I would like to straighten up my equipment."

So Smith and I remained in the Science Room, alone together. I pulled a stool up to the table, moved the magnifying apparatus aside, and looked at the book with my naked eye.

Why is there writing, and drawing, on only one side? I asked myself, turning pages back and forth absentmindedly.

Why is the text apparently nonsense?

Why did I risk my career only to lose Leah?

And why am I thinking about Leah right now, of all times?

I chuckled to myself, for some reason just then remembering how easily she had seen through my football-score prank, how she had—

I turned the book upside down. That is, I rotated it 180 degrees, so that the blank pages were now on my right, rather than my left. Because my left eye doesn't work, I had been seeing the decorated pages clearly, but almost entirely to the exclusion of the blank pages. Almost entirely, I say, because something on those pages was registering in my brain only without my realizing it.

I moved the magnifying glass back over the book and confirmed my suspicion. The blank pages were *not* entirely blank.

"Smith! Look at this!"

Smith joined me at the table, and I showed him that on each otherwise unmarked page was a marking, of one kind or another, in one or more corners of the page. They were small, and faint, but they were there, and they were the key. They had to be.

"It's a puzzle," I said. But what kind of puzzle? Did each marking have a different meaning? Was it a code? Did the meaning of the mark depend on what corner of the page it was in? Was a circle in the top left corner different from a circle on the bottom right, or did a triad of wavy lines have the same import as that same icon elsewhere?

"Zusammensetzspiel?" Smith said with a chuckle of his own.

Jigsaw puzzle. Yes! Not a code, but a physical puzzle.

"Smith," I said, "you're a genius. How many pages are in this book?" I asked, but I wasn't actually asking. I was about to count.

"One hundred ninety-six," Smith said, and when I gave him a dubious look he said with a shrug, "I counted earlier, when you flipped through them."

"One hundred ninety-six," I repeated. "Is that—?"

"Fourteen squared," Smith confirmed my new suspicion.

"Smith," I told him, "I need a scalpel. Do you have a scalpel?" But he was already handing me one.

"Oh, no, no, no," Guilmard said when he, Sanderson, and Iris returned and saw what Smith and I had done. "What did you do?!" Sanderson asked.

"It was completely necessary," Smith reported.

"The pages of the book hold the answer to... something," I said. "Even if we don't know what, exactly. In any event, I discovered how to unlock the answer. How to get us closer to unlocking it, anyway. I apologize for mangling metaphors. Also for carving up the book, but the pages were bound in order to hide their proper arrangement," I explained. "The leaves are meant to be joined two-dimensionally." I pointed out the markings on the backs of the pages, all of which were now spread out, face-down, on the large table. "We need to match up the markings so that the sheets form a fourteen-by-fourteen rectangle."

Even Guilmard was convinced by my explanation. Or, if he wasn't, he didn't protest. He and the others immediately got to work helping me arrange the 196 pages now liberated from their binding into the appropriate alignment.

When we had done this, and when we had applied an obscene amount of cellophane tape to the juxtaposed edges, nothing happened. Nothing magical, anyway. Nothing obvious. Not even when we turned the giant mosaic over again so that it was illuminated-side-up.

"Maybe we're... I don't know," Iris said. "Too close to it?"

"That's not crazy," I said. "Can we..." I looked around. "Can we hang it on a wall? There." I pointed to one side of the lab. "Let's get it up there. Maybe it will look like something from across the room."

But it didn't. The text was beyond illegible at that distance, and the illustrated scenes were barely discernible. There just wasn't anything to see at any scale. And, unlike earlier, my being half-sighted wasn't helping me see what we were all missing.

Maybe, I thought, it wasn't something to be seen. I don't know why I thought that, but in any event, I walked over to the hanging tapestry, closed my eyes, and put my hand to the papers. What was I expecting to feel? It felt like... paper. Sturdy paper, to be sure. Mostly smooth—almost entirely smooth, really. I didn't think I could feel the ink, but every so often as I ran my hand across the leaves, I thought I felt something that felt... different. Maybe a little stickier, or a little grittier.

"Iris?" I called. "What's my finger on? Right here?"

I heard Iris walk over to me, and then I heard her say, "The Sun."

Without opening my eyes, I moved my finger around until I felt another stickier, grittier spot. "Now?" I asked.

"Another Sun," Iris said. "Carp, are you fooling around?"

I said I wasn't, and then I heard the other men join us at the array. Once more without looking I fingered a sun. Satisfied, I opened my eyes.

The suns in the illuminations—the only thing they had in common, and every *single illustrated scene had a sun*—were different. The suns were the key.

"Now, *why* do they feel different?" I asked.

Iris was already scraping ink from one onto a glass Petri dish.

"Sanderson?" Iris said, but he was already holding open the door to the room. They stepped out, to another lab in the facility, I presumed.

"Puzzles upon puzzles," Smith remarked.

"I'm sorry about the book," I said to Guilmard.

"Don't be, Carp," he replied. "What you've uncovered is ingenious, and you've uncovered it ingeniously."

"If by that you mean entirely by accident," I said, "then I thank you kindly."

"Gentlemen," Iris announced, bursting back into the room, Sanderson right behind her.

"What is it?" I asked.

"It's organic," Iris said.

"Meaning?"

"Chemically speaking," Iris said, "it means that it contains carbon, and that it's of biological origin."

"Biological?" I asked. "It's alive?"

"No," Sanderson said, "but it was. It's a compound derived from bacteria."

"And what does that tell us?"

"That alone," Sanderson said, "doesn't tell us much. But the kind of bacteria the compound was likely derived from has a peculiar property, and that does tell us something very important. It's bioluminescent."

"It—"

But before I could ask *It glows in the dark?* someone—Smith, it would turn out—flipped the light switch in the Science Room, which should have plunged us into complete darkness, but didn't, quite, because once the fluorescent lamps were extinguished, the multiple suns of the canvas glowed like so many... well, stars.

And that's just what we all, as one, realized they were meant to be. *Stars.*

We were looking at a map of the night sky. And it was beautiful. It was the awe-inspiring night sky that one could never see from the streets of Manhattan, or even the outer boroughs. One had to leave the city, travel to somewhere remote like the Catskills, for instance. And when one stared at a sky like that, even with only one good eye, one could not help but be filled with an overwhelming sense of—

"Those are not our stars," Sanderson said.

"Hm?" I asked.

"He is correct," Smith said. "None of the constellations visible from Earth, in either hemisphere, is there."

"You don't say," I said, but distractedly. I realized that I was staring at one of the stars more than the others, I think because that one star was shining a little bit more brightly than the others. I knew that I should be frustrated, having not quite solved the puzzle at hand, but for the moment I was ineffably happy to be looking at a sky full of stars, whichever ones they might be. If this was it, if this was the end of the adventure, then at least it was easy on the eye.

(EARLY DECEMBER ONE LAST TIME...)

The morning of the hearing had been dark. When Sammy and I had left our hotel, the sun hadn't quite begun to rise, but at least there had been the promise—the possibility, anyway—of sunshine and blue skies. When we finally exited the building where the hearing was held, it was obvious that such promise had been an illusion. The day was firmly gray and miserable. Mine was, for sure. Maybe Sammy saw it differently.

"Jeremiah?" he asked. "Are you okay?"

"I've been better, Sammy," I said. "That was not my finest hour."

"It was actually three hours. Officially."

"Time flies when you're being made to look like a complete idiot, I guess."

"I won't lie to you, Jeremiah. Your... remarks were not the most... coherent."

"No? Because to my ears they sounded like total nonsense," I told Sammy. "So 'not the most coherent' is actually a compliment."

"Do you really know that guy by reputation only?" He meant Guilmard. "He seemed to have a personal bone to pick with you."

"It did seem like that," I said, "didn't it?"

I must have gotten lost in thought because Sammy soon asked again, "Jeremiah?"

"What's up, Sammy?"

"I'm not going to head back to New York right away," he told me. "There's a lot here I'd like to see, and, as I said, business will be dead until after New Year's."

"You're staying?"

"For a few days, I think," Sammy said. "Why don't you stick around with me? We can be strangers in this strange land together."

I forced myself to focus on what Sammy was saying, which was not at all easy, as my mind just would not leave that hearing chamber. *What had happened in there?*

Just then, though, my cousin was asking me to postpone my own return to New York, to stay in Washington with him, to take in the sights. Did he want us to get to know each other better? We were family, yet we'd seen each other only twice in twenty years. Or did he think that a vacation, such as it was, would do me some good, my life back in New York not being anything worth rushing back to? Or both?

"Sammy," I said, "thanks. For the invitation, I mean, but also for all of your help. I really do appreciate it. I think I need to go back home, though. This afternoon. I... I don't think I would enjoy staying here any longer, and I'm sure I wouldn't be pleasant company right now, either," I said. "But I think I would very much enjoy having a cup of coffee with you back in New York, maybe even next week. How about that? Coffee next week in the City, Sammy?"

"All right, Jeremiah. It's a deal," Sammy said. "Listen, take care of yourself, okay? I know things aren't looking so great at the moment, but the worst is probably over. Go home, get a good night's sleep, treat yourself to a shave in the morning, and then maybe..." Sammy trailed off, but I knew what he was thinking.

I shook my lawyer cousin's hand. "Enjoy the sights, Sammy. Pick out a good souvenir and put it on my tab."

The worst was not over.

The train ride back to Jersey City was uneventful. I don't think I spoke to a single person—nor did I suspect that anyone was trying to communicate with me surreptitiously. Nobody talked to me, and I imagined it was because they all knew about the hearing, which of course they didn't, and probably never would. A single, three-hour Senate subcommittee meeting couldn't possibly be the sort of thing about which word spread quickly, or at all. In reality, the members of the subcommittee were unlikely even to mention the morning's proceedings to their own wives.

Soon enough I was getting off the train and onto a bus, and soon enough after that I was back in Columbus Circle, happy to be in Manhattan once again. I was a mostly broken man, but at least I was in my element. My city, anyway. Where I knew just where to find a good cup of coffee. I stepped into just such a place and dropped myself onto a stool at the counter. Waiting for a mug of the strong stuff, I idly thumbed through an open newspaper at my elbow. When I didn't see anything worth reading, I closed the paper.

The headline caught my eye, and something caught in my throat. Many things, it felt like.

CONSPIRA-B-C!
Prof. Gets Letters of Discredit

This was the *Post.* The evening edition. And, yes, I was the "Prof." in question, a quick skim of the article told me. I looked around for other papers. Where there were *Posts,* there were bound to be *Newses* as well. I found one—I pretty much yanked it from another patron's hands—and saw this:

PAY-E-I-O-U-LA!
Feds Stop Silly Syllabary

No! A syllabary is not the same as an alphabet, I thought, for not even my commingled shame and rage could displace my frustration with confusion of terms of my art.

"Does anyone have the *Times?*!" I shouted aloud.

Three or four people yelled "Quarter to seven" at me.

"Not the time!" I hollered at everyone in the restaurant. *The Times! The New York Goddamned Times!*"

"Buddy," a cook said, brandishing a greasy spatula, "settle down. There's a newsstand right outside."

I put a quarter on the counter and bolted out onto the sidewalk. At a kiosk on the corner of the block I found a stack of the Gray Lady herself, the paper of record of not just New York City but the country, an institution-in-print. And I was horrified to see this on Page One:

ACADEMIC TESTIFIES TO CONGRESS REGARDING GREAT VOWEL GRIFT; SPELLS END OF PUBLIC DECEPTION

I did not buy a copy.

I wish I could report that the following morning I'd awoken to discover that the "events" of the previous "week" or so had been nothing more than an elaborate, verisimilar nightmare— and that all was suddenly, wonderfully back to "normal." Alas, when I opened my eyes (yes, I open both—if I could keep the bad one closed all the time, I wouldn't need a patch) everything was just as bad as it had been when I'd gone to bed the night before and considered never again getting out of it.

And it was only ten short minutes before things got even worse.

A telegram arrived to inform me that my employment at and by Dreyfus College had come to an end. (Western Union, no less. At least I wasn't fired on the cheap.)

YOUR SERVICES NO LONGER NEEDED
YOUR OFFICE TO BE PACKED UP AND DELIVERED
A GROSSMAN ESQ

Even though the communiqué had been subscribed by the school's lawyer, I knew that the decision to terminate me had been made by the appropriate faculty committee and confirmed, promptly and necessarily, by President Miller, who must have been shown one newspaper or another, or all of them. He could have protected me from myself and delayed the inevitable only so far and for so long. And thus, so long it was. So long, academia. See you again maybe never.

I looked into my icebox, cabinets, and cupboards, taking stock of my provisions. I figured I could stay holed up inside for a full three days, as long as I didn't get so bored that I decided to see how much I could eat in one sitting.

Three days with nothing but your regrets to keep you company is a long time.

Do you know how many times in three days you can revisit every mistake you made that led you to be hiding in your apartment for three days?

And do you know how much good it does?

And do you have any idea how quickly you'll get tired of listening to yourself talk? And how frustrating it is to know the punch lines to all of your own jokes?

Eventually I had to leave my apartment. I had to venture out into the cold, uncaring world. Perhaps it wasn't fair of me to think of the world as uncaring—but December in New York City was cold. I bundled up well.

And then I just walked. I had no destination in mind. I walked whichever way was convenient. Maybe I would get lost. Maybe I would walk until my hat floated. Maybe...

Actually, there was no maybe about this: I was being followed. I don't even know how I knew it, but I knew it. Someone was walking where I was walking, and since I wasn't walking anywhere specific, it was obvious that this other person wanted to be only where I was, just a few steps behind.

But why would anyone want to follow *me?* What did I have that anyone could have wanted? I didn't even have the things that I wanted anymore. What did the broken, miserable, unemployed shell of a one-eyed crypto-linguist have to offer anyone?

Maybe I was merely about to get mugged. I supposed it only made sense that I'd get mugged that morning too.

(AND, FINALLY, LATE DECEMBER...)

"We know where those stars are," a man announced.

"Or, we can figure out where they are, anyway," a second man clarified.

These two men were who we needed to make sense of everything laid out before us, and they had just arrived at Area 50. With Bradford, of course.

"Everyone," Bradford said, "this is Allan Green and Alan Little."

"We've met," I remarked.

"Professor Carp," Little said. "We're very sorry about what you've been through."

"What we put you through," said Green. "But there's no denying that you've been instrumental in solving an eons-old mystery."

"Have I?" I asked, and I wasn't being sarcastic.

"Of course!" Little insisted.

"Thanks to you," Green explained, "we now know why The Gramideon failed to unite Humanity the first time it appeared on Earth."

"You know why?" Guilmard asked.

"We do," Green assured us all.

"It didn't," Little said, confusing us all again. "The Gramideon did just what it was intended to do, in fact. It just didn't work quite the way the Cosmic Etymistics of Insignia Gamma expected, or wanted."

"The who of what?" Sanderson, the astrobiologist, asked.

"The Cosmic Etymistics of Insignia Gamma," Little said, "are a primordial race of beings with a truly venerable power. They forged The Gramideon and instilled in it its unifying force, then sent it to Earth a very long time ago."

"When it arrived here," Green continued, "its quality of self-inference convinced Humans to accept it, and once accepted, it worked to reshape Human temperament, to reduce the Human predispositions toward distrust and aggression, to stimulate and cultivate compromise, helpfulness, teamwork."

"Cooperation," I said. "That's just what Vister said."

"Vister!" Green exclaimed.

"Vister... was here?" Little asked.

"Not *here*. But here on Earth, yes. He abducted me. Briefly."

"That's troubling," Green confided in us.

"But not actually problematic. Vister knows that The Gramideon has lost its power," Little said. "He doesn't know that we can re-energize it."

"So to speak," Green felt it necessary to add.

"Lost its power?" Iris asked.

"So to speak?" I asked.

"The creations of the Cosmic Etymistics lose potency when left dormant for long enough, as The Gramideon was here on Earth," Little said. "Which happened once the peoples of Earth had fully cooperated."

"They had?" Smith asked. "When? And to what end?"

"Not long after they received The Gramideon," Green answered Smith, "and it began working, Humans realized that they were being manipulated."

"Just as Silas and I theorized!" Guilmard crowed.

"Indeed," Little agreed. "Humanity ultimately rejected the influence that was bringing it together as a race..."

"...and that very influence allowed disparate peoples to work together to remove The Gramideon—and all traces of it—from Earth."

We were all quiet for a good minute before anyone spoke again.

"But you said you can... revitalize the Gramideon?" Sanderson asked.

"The Cosmic Etymistics can. And we have every confidence that they will, if we ask them to," said Green. "Nicely. If we use the Magic Word, which they also created."

"We just didn't know where to find them," said Little.

"You don't know..." I began.

"...where Insignia Gamma is?" Little finished for me. "As I said, we *didn't* know. The Universe is a very large place."

"And the Cosmic Etymistics are rumored to be a very reclusive race," Green added, as if they were collaborating on a poem.

"But now we do know where to go to petition them," Little said, pointing at the celestial atlas we'd assembled, and specifically at the one star that shone a little brighter than the others. "There."

We all turned to look at the star map, and a reverential, reflective silence fell over the room.

Then Green asked, "You don't mind if we borrow that, do you?"

"By all means," Guilmard spoke for the group, and humanity for that matter.

"I have just one more question," Iris said before Allan and Alan departed Earth for Insignia Gamma. "The shards. You made those?" The trunk that Sanderson and Guilmard had brought from England had been moved out into the hallway, I saw, which probably meant that Allan and Alan would be taking it with them.

"A member of our team did," Little said, a bit reticently. "Yes."

"We have a team back on Alstromeria," Green mentioned, "not unlike yours here."

"The craftsmanship is exquisite," Iris remarked. "My compliments to the smithy."

"We'll pass that along when we catch up to him," Little said.

"Catch up to him?" I asked. "You don't mean..."

Green confirmed my suspicion. "I do. Vister made the shards. And he planted them on Earth. And then he sabotaged the entire mission."

"Why?" I asked.

"Because he's a jerk," Little said.

"Every race has jerks," Green told us.

"So," I said to the group, once it was just us Earthlings again and we had turned the lights back on, "is that it, then? For now, anyway?"

"Well," Sanderson said, "we do have to find a way to insinuate Glyph Two-Six—"

"The Gramideon," I said.

"Aitch," Guilmard put in, smiling at me.

"—into the Modern Roman alphabet," Sanderson finished.

"So that humanity can avoid being put out of its misery by more enlightened races in the Universe who think we're too uncivilized to share space with them," Iris added.

"Supposedly," Smith remarked.

"That would seem to be the task at hand," Bradford confirmed.

"Okay, then, Bradford," I said. "What are our marching orders?"

"Carp," Bradford said, "we've known each other for a full two weeks now. Haven't you figured out yet what my particular skill is?"

"You're very good at not answering questions," I said. "Is it that?"

"I bring people together," Bradford told me. "Specifically, I bring the right people together. Usually the first step is finding the right people. Fortunately, I have an aptitude for that as well."

I considered this, and, reflecting on the prior two weeks, realized that Bradford was correct.

"You're a matchmaker!"

"I suppose."

"Where I come from, Bradford, that's an honorable, admirable, full-time profession, but one attempted by only the most talented practitioners. You could make good money in my community."

"I'm perfectly happy with my present employment," Bradford said. "But I might be inclined to do a colleague a personal favor in that regard. As an expression of my gratitude for his help."

I didn't know what to say.

"You're talking about me, right?" I asked. "You're saying you'd try to help me patch things up with Leah?"

"Yes, Carp."

"Leah is my ex-fiancée," I told the others. "She broke off our engagement after I lost my job when the hoax was exposed."

The others murmured sympathetically. But I also thought I heard a soft cough, and out of the corner of my eye I saw Iris shaking her head, as if to say *no*.

"No?" I asked her.

"No," she said.

"No what?" I asked.

"No, you cannot have Bradford—or anyone else, for that matter—plead your case to the woman you love."

"That's too bad," I lamented. "Leah doesn't want to talk to me."

"Of course she wants to talk to you! Carp, I might be just a simple country archaeometallurgist, but I happen to know a thing or two about women. So trust me when I tell you that your ex-fiancée does not want to be your ex-fiancée. She just needs you to give her a reason to say yes again. But it has to be you who gives her that reason."

"But nothing has changed!" I protested. I wanted Iris to be right, but the reason Leah had broken off our engagement still held. It didn't matter that I had helped save the world.

"Yes, it will," Smith said.

"What will?" I asked. Had he read my mind?

"It will matter that you're helping to save the world. Won't it, Iris?"

"In her shoes, I'd certainly take it into consideration," Iris said. "But you probably don't want to make a big deal of it, either."

I was thinking about that when something occurred to me. It dawned on me what else Bradford had just been telling me, and the others as well.

"You're moving on. Your work here is done. You've brought this group together, and now it's up to us to continue the mission... without you."

Bradford nodded.

"But," I asserted, "we need a leader."

"Have you ever led a top secret team, Carp?" Bradford asked me.

"I can't say that I have," I replied, seeing where he was going.

"Then it won't be you," Bradford said. "Doctor Lucas will be in charge."

I spent New Year's Eve with my mother. It was fine, but I went to bed and was asleep well before midnight. By choice. Recent events, I realized, had exhausted me.

The following day—January 1, 1949—I was back in my own place, finally able to start opening the dozens of boxes that had been delivered by my former employer. The contents of my office. After opening several, it occurred to me that I really did not have anywhere in my apartment to put the hundreds of books I had accumulated over the years—accumulated with abandon, since I could store them in my office at the college and because the college paid for almost all of them—so I changed my activity to just moving all of the boxes out of the way. I located a handful of favorite volumes and dropped them onto the desk in my study. In doing that, I knocked over the souvenir my cousin Sammy had brought me from Washington: a novelty pewter replica of the Capitol with a pencil sharpener embedded in it. The thing was undeniably tacky, and I believed that Sammy knew as much when he picked it out for me.

When I picked it up, I noticed that the United States Capitol, when viewed from above, looks not unlike... no, that's too far-fetched. It doesn't really. It's an architectural coincidence, nothing more. Even if the building where the legislative branch of the government of one of the planet's political superpowers meets regularly would be an excellent place to have cooperation promoted...

There was a knock on my apartment door. I wasn't expecting company, but I supposed I might enjoy some adult conversation. It was that or sharpening some pencils.

I opened the door to find Leah standing at the threshold.

"Oh," I said. "Hi."

"Hi."

"Come... come in. Please. Please come in." *Eloquent to the last, Jeremiah.*

Leah came in. I offered her a seat. I made us a fresh pot of tea.

"You wanted to tell me something—," Leah started to say.

But then my phone rang.

"I'm so sorry," I told Leah. "Let me just see who that is?"

Suddenly I was very popular. Almost too popular.

"Doctor Miller... yes. Thank you, sir. And to you as well. Yes, of course. Of course I'd be willing to discuss my return to Dreyfus," I said. Then, looking over at Leah waiting to talk about the recent past—and maybe *our* future—I said, "But I'm afraid I'm going to have to call you back." I hung up the phone.

"You were saying...?" I asked Leah.

"I was saying that you asked me to come over to talk, and you said on the phone that you had something to tell me about saving the world. So I'm here. But, Jeremiah, please don't lie to me."

"Leah," I said, "I promise that as long as you're willing to listen to me, I will never, ever lie to you." And I held out a hand for her to shake on that deal.

"A handshake, Jeremiah?" she asked, and when we embraced instead, she pinched me somewhere tender.

"Aitch!" I exclaimed.

"What?"

"I said *ouch.*"

AFTERWORD

The germ of this novel was an unpublished 1,609-word humor piece in the form of an interview with an ancient resident of the Achy Shtetl Rest Home—the man whose life had taken a hard left turn decades earlier when he'd agreed to help invent an addition to the Roman alphabet: Jeremiah Carp, father of the letter H.

In that original piece, "The Great Vowel Grift," Carp was not just very old but very angry, and with good reason: He'd never been redeemed. He'd gone off a glyph and then been put out to pasture, with years upon years of half-blind hindsight to haunt him. When I had the idea to explore his character and exploits in a novel, though, I knew I'd have to give Carp an opportunity for vindication. And I figured I'd have to give him a more compelling reason to risk everything for a prank, even if the hijinks were highbrow. I settled on aliens. As one does.

The Vowels of the Earth sat for a while. I completed the manuscript in September of 2016, then put it aside to write seven more novels (including three for younger readers) and to collaborate with my wife on a picture book (also, for that matter, on a second child).

Ironically, when newly-minted editor-in-chief of Humorist Books Brian Boone reached out to me in the summer of 2023 and asked if I had any humorous novels to offer for consideration, Vowels was the last of my manuscripts to come to mind. When finally it did, however, I remembered that Brian himself had read it when I'd first written it—and he'd loved it. I reminded him as much... and now here we are: me, the proud author of a published novel; you, with that novel in your hands for a few moments more; and Brian, half-asleep in an easy chair, nursing a tumbler of 30-year-old Scotch (tape, not whiskey), listening to John Mellencamp's "Dance Naked" on repeat.

Brian's insane, is what I'm getting at. But he knows what he's doing, and among the several people who have stuck their necks out for me, I owe him—and Humorist Books publisher Marty Dundics—especial gratitude. Thank you, gentlemen. If I could invent a new letter (or two) in your honor, I would.

Matthew David Brozik
February 2024

Jeremiah Carp will return in *A World Without N*

ABOUT THE AUTHOR

Matthew David Brozik loves letters enough to use them almost every day.

Made in the USA
Monee, IL
14 May 2024

58402970R00111